The Heart of Hyndorin

Modern Magick, 8

Charlotte E. English

Copyright © 2019 by Charlotte E. English

All rights reserved.

No portion of this book may be reproduced in any form without written permission from the publisher or author, except as permitted by EU copyright law.

1

10:38AM ON A BRIGHT, shiny day in July (I'd lost track of the date), and I was beginning to get a deep sense of déjà vu.

'The Hyndorin Mountains,' I had said to about thirty-eight passers-by in succession, and received the same response from all of them: a puzzled frown and a shake of the head. 'Sorry,' they said. 'Never heard of it.'

Which is pretty much exactly what happened a couple of days ago, when we went in search of the Vales of Wonder.

'Maybe it's just so far from Scarborough that the people here don't know it,' I said, stopping on a sunny street corner.

But Jay shook his head. 'Someone ought to have at least heard the name before. We're getting nothing but total incomprehension.'

I sighed. 'Which means what, it's had a name change? Like Vale?'

'Could be.'

'Or,' said Emellana Rogan, my idol, 'It is either inaccessible or it no longer exists.'

Why is it that the voice of reason always has to be so depressing?

'It must exist,' I objected. 'Mountain ranges don't just disappear.'

'Is it a mountain range? Whatever Torvaston considered of interest in those parts, it cannot have been simply a piece of topography. Perhaps it was a town. Or an area within a wider mountain range, which can no longer be reached, and has therefore faded from public knowledge.'

'Either way,' said Miranda, 'asking around doesn't seem to be helping much.'

Quite right, we were wasting time. But coming from Miranda, who summarily failed to follow up her observation with a useful suggestion, I found it nettling.

'Right,' I said, hiding my irritation. 'We could be looking for a piece of history, then. Fortunately, we're good at that.'

'To the library?' said Jay, perking up.

'To the nearest library, and post-haste.' I asked the next passer-by for directions to the library, instead of the Hyndorin Mountains, and received a much more satisfactory reply.

'Second to the left, and straight on till morning?' said Jay.

'I knew it was a good idea to bring the navigator.'

Jay bowed.

'Alternatively, next street over on the right, around the corner, and across the road.'

'Reality is always so prosaic.'

'I know,' I said, patting Jay's arm. 'It's disappointing.'

I tried not to notice the way he flinched when I touched him, just as I'd tried not to notice that the others were surreptitiously giving me a wide berth.

'Sorry,' said Jay, noticing me noticing. 'It's just that it—'

'Feels like a shot of pure bliss directly to the heart?' I said hopefully.

'More like an electric shock straight to the brain.'

'I'll work on that.'

The problem was, I was overflowing with magick. Ever since *someone* had put that wretched lyre into my hands, up at the top of the town of Vale. You know, right where its ancient magick was at its most potent.

It and I might since have parted ways, but I'd managed to take quite a lot of the magick with me. Or something. Whether I'd simply absorbed a small ocean of the stuff and failed to discharge it (making me a walking magickal battery), or whether I'd become some kind of magickal generator (like the griffins), was still under question.

I couldn't tell. I just knew that every cell of my body buzzed with potential, like I could move mountains if I wanted to. The few, small experiments I'd ventured to perform (over the long, long night while everyone else slept, and I couldn't), had demonstrated that I was indeed more magickally adept than I'd ever been before.

Something up there in Vale had supercharged me.

I wasn't sure I approved. And the farther we got from Vale, where I had felt more or less on a level with my surroundings, the less sure I was. I certainly couldn't go home in this state.

I hoped I wasn't condemned to a lifetime of exile.

Libraries, though. Libraries are soothing. The moment we stepped through the big glass doors of the-fifth-Scarborough's public library (leaving Pup on the doorstep, prudently tied to the railing), I felt subtly eased. The mere sight of all those books calmed me down. Hey, if I couldn't have human touch, I could still have reading.

Hopefully. I did sometimes have an odd effect on inanimate objects, too.

The four of us paused on the threshold, taking in the feast of knowledge before us in appreciative silence. Not a bad sized library, considering that Scarborough isn't a particularly large town. A big, airy room stretched before us, bookshelves arranged in neat rows across its floor, and all around the walls. Everything was neatly organised and labelled, just the way I like it.

I spotted a sign reading "history", and made a beeline for it.

'Right, Mauf,' I said, hauling his huge bookly form out of my satchel. 'All our hopes depend on you.'

'Ouch,' said Mauf.

I quickly set him down on the nearest table. 'Great. Even my favourite book recoils from my touch.'

Mauf ruffled his pages, perhaps pleased with my shameless piece of flattery. 'Dear Miss Vesper, never would I *recoil* from you.'

'You'd suffer my proximity bravely, heroically, and without complaint, because you love me?'

'Quite.'

'I appreciate that.'

Mauf smiled bookishly. 'What is it that I may do for you this morning, madam?'

'We're looking for those Hyndorin Mountains. You may recall, the ones on the scroll-case map.'

'I recall it perfectly. Indeed, I retain a copy of the map in question.'

'I thought you might. I don't suppose the map has any hidden hints as to how to get there?' It was always possible that Mauf might discern something undetectable to our feeble human perceptions.

'I am afraid not. The map appears more along the lines of a memorandum than a practical guide, and contains no instruction as to how to reach it from any particular part of Britain.'

Curse it.

'In that case, we rely on these shelves for information. Can you... search the books, somehow, for any mention of Hyndorin?'

'Hyndorin anything,' put in Jay. 'As Em said, it might not be a mountain range. And by this time, four centuries after Torvaston drew the map, it could be anything at all.'

'Like an inaccessible ruin,' I said.

'Including that.'

'It will take some time,' said Mauf.

'Why don't I wait here with Mauf,' said Jay, taking a seat at the table. 'Ves, you and Em could ask the library staff to check the catalogue?'

Me and Em, huh? I could almost swear Jay winked at me, like a match-making Mama out of some historical romance.

Had I made my girl crush so very obvious? Oops.

'What about Mir—' I began, in the smoothest subject change ever, but as I spoke I noticed her on the other side of the library, pulling books off the shelves. The sign over her head read "Zoology", so that was her occupied for the next twelve years or so.

Away went Em and I to the librarian's desk, me labouring to exude the kind of coolness Em achieved without effort.

'Do you, um, have any other ideas?' I tried.

'Our current course of action is precisely what I would do myself.'

I felt an irrational little glow at what amounted to clear approval, and felt like an idiot. What was I, seven, and delighted with a word of praise from the teacher? *Grown woman, Ves,* I reminded myself, with as much effect as usual.

The librarian proved to be of the troll peoples; she and Em surveyed each other with obvious satisfaction.

'Good morning,' said Em. 'We're after information about the Hyndorin Mountains.'

The librarian, inevitably, looked blank. 'Geography is at the back, on the right.'

'We're in a bit of a hurry,' I said. 'Could you maybe check if there's anything listed in the catalogue?'

She did. There wasn't.

'Fiction's that way,' she said, pointing.

'It definitely isn't fiction. It's marked on a map drawn a few centuries ago.'

Scepticism joined the befuddled look. 'We've a mythology section. Perhaps there's something in there.'

Demoted in a single sentence from serious scholars to dreamers on the trail of Atlantis. I stifled a sigh, thanked her, and drifted away.

But Em did not. 'Do you perhaps have any reference titles on the mountains of the British Isles?' she said.

'Oh, certainly.' A few minutes' work with an enormous enchanted tome — I did rather like these magickal computers — and she had a list of two titles for us. These she wrote down on a slip of paper, which she handed to Em with a smile. 'Good luck,' she said, ignoring me entirely.

Comes of being short, I suppose.

We soon tracked down the books. 'Let's get these to Gallimaufry,' she said, handing one to me. *The Peaks of Britain,* it called itself, and a flick through revealed a reasonable quantity of promising maps and discussion, some of them hand-drawn and pleasantly elderly-looking.

Jay sat with Mauf open on his lap, his back to the room. 'Any luck?' I said, taking the seat next to him — and drawing it a safe distance away. 'We've got these.'

'Not much,' said Jay, taking a cursory glance at my book.

'No one can report any instance of the word "Hyndorin" appearing anywhere in this library,' said Mauf, and I realised that by "no one" he meant the books. 'Nor anything similar.'

'Curse it.'

'Indeed. But there are two references to hidden mountain enclaves. Neither of them are detailed, nor are they from sources that might be termed properly academic. Mere hearsay.'

'Old stories have often been our ally,' I objected. 'Hearsay sometimes has some truth lurking behind it.'

'Nor does this seem so very far-fetched,' said Em. 'After all, even our own world, diminished as it is, retains a fair number of hidden magickal enclaves.'

Mauf sniffed. 'I *did* say that neither was detailed. One speaks vaguely of Derbyshire. The other refers only to "the Peaks".'

I sat up a bit. 'But in our Britain, there's a Peak District *in* Derbyshire, sometimes referred to simply as the Peaks.' I leafed furiously through the book Em had handed me, and found a whole chapter devoted to the subject. *Score.*

'Especially by locals,' said Jay. 'Who wrote that book, Mauf?'

'It is unattributed. The book is at least a hundred years old, as far as I am able to determine, and appears to consist of a collection of somebody's annotated explorations.'

'Did the author get into this supposed mountain enclave?' I said.

'No.'

'Mmpf. Well, it's better than nothing.'

'It might be a lot worse than nothing,' said Jay. 'If it proves to be irrelevant.'

'True. But we aren't getting very far looking for references to these Hyndorin Mountains that don't seem to exist, at least not around here. I vote we go down to Derbyshire and look around. Maybe we can dig up something more useful.'

'I don't have a better idea,' said Jay, which was support of a kind.

Em gave me a slow nod, which I hoped meant "this, also, is exactly what I would do." I beamed.

'You about finished, Mauf?' I said.

'I do not believe there is anything more of use to be gleaned here,' he said, with some disdain.

So much for the Scarborough Public Library. Mauf was so hard to please. 'Ok, let's go,' I said.

But as I pushed back my chair, Miranda reappeared, carrying a big cloth-bound reference book. She dropped this onto the table before us; it landed with a *bang,* and a puff of dust. 'Look,' she said.

The cover was blank, but when I opened it up, the words *The Care and Breeding of Magickal Familiars* leapt out at me from the title page.

2

'Familiars?' I said, looking up at Miranda. 'Isn't that an outlawed art at home?'

'Not quite. It's strictly regulated, to the point that it might as well be banned as far as most people are concerned. Reason being, people are stupid. They try to take on creatures of far greater magickal potency than they can handle. The beast suffers, and the owner probably ends up as mincemeat.' Miranda's tone indicated her utter lack of sympathy for the latter.

'Okay, so it isn't a banned art here,' I said, leafing through the book.

Miranda took it off me, and opened it up at a chapter headed: *Griffins.*

'Griffin Familiars?' I squeaked. 'How's that possible?'

'I don't know if it still *is*, even here,' said Miranda. 'This book's eighty years old. But it *was*.'

'It is an art still practiced in some countries beyond Britain,' Em offered. 'Even with the greater beasts.' She looked at me in a thoughtful way that, for some reason, made me uneasy. 'Ves, some would say your relationship with Adeline is a form of Familiar-bonding.'

'Pup, too,' said Miranda. 'Or at least, that's where it's going.'

I may have blanched. 'But, um, that's illegal.'

'Not if you're properly regulated and acting with due authority,' said Miranda.

'But I'm not.'

'Want to bet?' said Jay. 'You think Milady isn't on top of all that?'

'Um.' I looked at Miranda. 'That lirrabird. Is that a familiar?'

'I'm building such a bond. It's... easier, here.'

Of course it was easier around here. It would be.

I thought about that.

'Why is this relevant?' said Jay to Miranda.

She scowled. 'I'm not sure if it is. But since everything about this little adventure keeps coming back to griffins, it could be useful to know.'

'It really could,' I said. 'Thank you.'

With a curt nod, she withdrew, taking the book with her.

'We're going back to the henge complex, right?' said Jay, fixing me with the eyes of hope.

'It does seem the quickest way to travel a few counties south.'

Jay rocketed out of his chair and was halfway to the door before I had time to draw breath.

I looked at Em. 'I think he likes that place.'

She smirked. 'What if I offered you a chocolate fountain the size of Stonehenge—'

'Say no more.' My eyes grew big.

'That's how Jay feels about those henge complexes.'

'In that case we'd better hurry, or we might never see him again.'

WE DIDN'T CATCH UP with Jay until we arrived at the gates of the henge complex. Whether he'd run all the way up the hill or just sprouted wings and flown, I couldn't have said. He stood a few feet short of the first of the stone circles, visibly impatient.

'Sorry,' I gasped as we came up. 'I haven't your stride. Or your deep lust for limitless Waytravel.'

'Got Addie?' he said, ignoring that.

'Kind of.' I tapped my bosom area, where my syrinx pipes lay safely hidden.

'Er.' Jay looked, and hastily looked away again. 'Is that a yes?'

'Don't ask me where she goes when she's not at my side, but she always comes when I whistle. And she's got to be safer wherever-that-is than trotting along at our heels.' We'd learned that the interesting way. Too many people took a greedy interest in my pretty Adeline.

Jay shrugged. 'Ok. She's your Familiar. Keep her wherever you like.'

'She's not—' I caught the twinkle of mischief in his eye, and abandoned my protest half-made. 'Fine.'

Jay had apparently had time to acquire travel tokens from the perambulatory kiosk, for he put one into my hand, and repeated the procedure with Em and Miranda. This one was cool to the touch and peculiarly incorporeal. I mean, I could see that a disk of something silvery lay in my palm, but all I could feel of it was a faint chill.

'Destination?' said Em.

'There's a major henge complex in Derby, seems to be the largest one in the area.'

'Derby may also have the largest library in the area, then,' said Em.

Jay nodded.

Pup writhed in my arms and tried to slither to the ground. I almost dropped both satchel and token, trying to hang onto her. 'Here,' I said, and handed her off to Em. I could've gentled her with a charm, but I don't like to do that to Goodie. It seems wrong to humble her mischievous little spirit just because it's inconvenient.

I suppose being forcibly detained by someone as large and inescapable as Em is much the same, as far as Pup's concerned.

Needs must.

'Come on.' Jay, bored with waiting for us to sort ourselves out, strode away. The three of us trailed obediently behind.

He made straight for a circle of stones of a kind I couldn't remember seeing before. A species of fluorite, if my gem-knowledge did not mislead me, with rough, alternating bands of misty-white and purple-blue. These had an airy delicacy about them which pleased me, not to mention their *most* attractive colour.

'These are nice,' I said as I stepped into the circle after Jay. 'What are they made o—'

Swoosh. The rest of my sentence dissolved into a shriek — more of surprise than fear, I swear. I was used to travelling with Jay, and it always took him a minute or so to muster up the Winds and orient himself, or whatever it was he did when he was preparing to go. But Waymastery in the henge complexes of the Fifth was instantaneous.

We reappeared, winded and speechless, in the midst of another such complex.

Jay had described it as the largest henge complex in the area; that in no way prepared me for the sheer hugeness of it. Scarborough's, impressive as it was, faded into insignificance in comparison. The complex must've been the size of a full football field, its surface intricately patterned with more henges than I wanted to try to count. Some of them were only about two feet across, large enough for a single person to travel through at a time.

Others... well. I tipped my head way, way back, trying to see the tops of a series of bloodstone pillars near the base of which we had emerged. The things must have been the height of a two-storey house, at least. The air bristled with jutting stones; sunlight glinted off a hundred different types of gem; and... *something* caught at my... everything, and pulled.

My left foot, I realised too late, had strayed into the edge of an alabaster circle. I don't normally feel these particular kinds of magicks; not being a Waymaster, I'm as oblivious to them as a deaf person is to Mozart's violin concertos.

This was different.

'Ah...' I said, filled with unease, as something deeply magickal about that henge-circle communed with something deeply magickal about me. 'This is not—'

I fell sideways, and vanished in a spray of magickal fireworks.

'*Jay...!*' I shrieked as the world upended around me.

I thought I heard cursing as I disappeared.

I *DEFINITELY* HEARD CURSING twelve seconds later.

When the world righted itself again and the nauseating blur faded from my eyes, I beheld the face of Jay, creased with annoyance. 'This,' he said, grabbing my hand in a vice-like grip, 'is going to prove *really* inconvenient.'

'This *what*?' I was set on my feet upright, and towed after Jay, who walked straight back into the nearest henge (lapis lazuli, very nice) without pause.

'This whatever is going on with you.' I detected a wince, but he didn't loose his hold on my hand.

'I find it a trifle inconvenient myse—' I began, but a rush of wind stole the rest of my words, as we vanished back into the Ways.

'No harm done?' said Emellana, seconds later. She and Miranda stood waiting with a placidity I might have found disconcerting, if I wasn't so busy catching my breath.

'She's in one piece.' Jay hadn't let go of my hand, and did not seem to have any plans to do so.

As a probable consequence of which, his eyes were changing colour again.

I decided not to tell him.

'Right, *now* we're going,' he said, and marched off, pulling me gently but firmly along behind him.

'Wait,' I said. 'What's going on? Am I a Waymaster now?'

'Did you do that intentionally?'

'No, but—'

'Then you aren't a Waymaster.'

'Then what am I—' I stopped dead, silenced, because unless I was crazy that was a familiar wide-brimmed hat vanishing into a milky labradorite henge about twenty feet ahead of us. 'Is that... no, surely it can't be.'

'It was,' said Jay grimly, and broke into a run. 'Come on!'

I didn't need much encouragement. That hat, with its distinctive curving shape, and floating as it had been about four feet from the floor, could only belong to our shady little "friend", Wyr. The one who'd tried to sell Adeline to the beast-traders of Vale.

The one who'd purloined Torvaston's scroll-case, and absconded with it.

I'd wondered at the time what he wanted with that item in particular, and hadn't been able to come up with an answer.

Well, apparently he was as desirous of finding the Hyndorin Mountains as we were. Was there something in those lost mountains that interested the sticky-fingered little creep? That interested *me* rather a lot.

'Em!' I shouted, stretching out my free hand behind me. 'Catch hold, and grab Mir. We're going to be—'

Travelling tokenless, I was going to say, which would mean we'd have to keep hold of Jay if we wanted to be taken along. But there wasn't time. Just as Em's large hand closed around my small one, Jay ran full-tilt into the embrace of those milk-white stones, and my breath escaped in a rush as we fell headlong into the Ways once again.

We came out somewhere higher up, if the chill in the air was anything to go by. A vast blue sky dotted with clouds stretched overhead; I glimpsed feathery grasses, and smelled summer flowers. Several henges were spread over the hillside even up here, though these were all of a less polished appearance: limestone or granite, white and dark, moss-grown and aged.

There was no sign of Wyr.

Jay stood, panting, and turned us in circles, hoping to spot something of the thief. 'Um,' he said. 'I can't tell where he's gone.'

'Em?' I said, kindly releasing her hand. I tried to detach myself from Jay, too, entirely for his benefit, but his fingers closed the more tightly on mine, until my bones creaked.

'Don't let go yet,' said Jay. 'Can't be sure you won't be swept away again.'

I abandoned my efforts with a small sigh. 'Em, can you tell which circle's been most recently used?'

Her eyes brightened, and she nodded. 'I think so,' she murmured, already in motion. 'There is a certain residue, like a brightness...' She dismissed a set of crumbling limestone blocks with a shake of her head, and shortly afterwards a taller series of dark, almost black granite stones. 'Ah,' she said then, pausing at the third. Humble, that one, to say the least: there were no stones visible, just a circuit of raised bumps in the grass. 'This one.'

'Sure?' said Jay, watching her with intent, moon-silver eyes.

I winced.

Em did her brisk, authoritative nod, the one I always found reassuring.

Jay apparently did, too, for he didn't hesitate. I had just time to grab hold of Emellana again and off we went, tumbling into the windy embrace of the modest, grassy henge.

On the other side, a wild, blasted heath awaited us, a landscape straight out of a Bronte novel. Not a scrap of greenery met my eyes, only tawny-brown scrub and bare earth. Huge boulders lay scattered about, haphazard; not henges, these, just socking great rocks. We were truly high up high, now; the wind whistled and howled past my ears, and around us stretched a rolling, rocky landscape bare of all signs of human habitation.

Well, almost. Someone had thoughtfully carved their names into the nearest of the gigantic boulders. *Rufus & June.* Nice touch.

I felt something shift, behind me. A disturbance, slight in truth, but prominent in my weirdly amplified state. I preferred to attribute my unseemly dizziness to the same source. I whirled, turning giddy in an instant, and contrived to fall heavily atop the small, scarcely-visible person attempting to slither unobtrusively away.

'Hello, Wyr,' I growled, catching hold of his jacket with both hands. 'I'd *really* like to talk to you.'

3

'THAT FEELING,' SAID WYR, attempting to writhe out of my grip, 'is not mutual.'

'That's too bad,' I said, handing him off to Emellana. He didn't stand much chance of getting away from *her*. 'What are you doing here? And where's our scroll-case?'

'I sold it,' he said, eyeing Em with distaste. 'Obviously. What else would I do with it?'

'Take an interest in a certain map that was drawn on it, by chance?'

'What map.'

'Ah. So your appearance up here is a coincidence.'

'Apparently.' He smiled at me, and flicked the brim of his hat.

I felt like sweeping that hat off him and hurling it (or him) off the peak.

'Look, this is not going to fly. You've some kind of interest in the Hyndorin Mountains, and if you don't speak up, Em's going to break you into pieces and feed you to the birds.' I'd seen a few large ones sailing overhead, birds of prey by the looks of them.

Wyr surveyed Emellana, unimpressed. 'She's big, but old ladies don't tend to scare— *argh!*'

I don't know what Em did, but obviously it hurt. She looked at him, cold as winter, and said, 'Talk.'

'I don't—' said Wyr, but this unpromising beginning was interrupted by a shimmer and a ripple of magick, emanating from the stony henge. Someone was coming through.

A tall figure appeared. Troll-tall, broad-shouldered, and achingly familiar. He paused only for a split second in the centre of the henge, and made as if to go away again — then saw me, and stopped dead. '*Ves.*'

A moment later, Baron Alban was bearing down on me with obvious intent to hug. Ruthlessly.

Remembering, in the nick of time, my uncuddleable state, I took a few hasty steps back. '*Alban*?' I said, in disbelief. 'Great. Now I'm hallucinating.'

'Nope,' said Jay succinctly.

Emellana smiled at the vision. 'Highness.'

'You're really here,' I said. 'How.'

Alban stopped a few feet from me, uncertainty replacing the relief on his face. 'Long story,' he said.

'It's not you,' I tried to explain, regretting my instinctive retreat. 'It's— uh, long story too.'

'All right.'

'You first?'

He sighed, and it struck me how weary he looked. In fact, he looked most unlike himself. He was clad in plain travelling clothes, devoid of ornaments, his head bare; the attractive, bluish-green tones of his skin and bronzed hair were gone, and he was merely brown-haired, with lightly tanned skin. It would be like me showing up in jeans and an old t-shirt, with my natural hair colour showing. 'Is everything all right?' I added.

'It is now,' he said, smiling at me, and he was the same old Alban again, even if rather less well turned-out. He looked around at Em and Jay and Miranda, and focused with a frown on Wyr. 'Since you all appear to be hale and in one piece... who's that?'

'Our nemesis,' I said. 'Apparently.'

Wyr, visibly more disconcerted by the Baron's presence than by Emellana's, said nothing.

To my dismay, Alban swayed on his feet, and quickly sat down — outside the range of the henge. He held up a hand as I started forward. 'Don't worry. I've just been through one too many henges today, that's all.'

'As in, how many?'

'As in, I've been travelling the Ways since last night trying to find you.'

'*All night*? Why? What's happened?'

'Nothing terrible,' he said, seeing the alarm in my face.
'Or at least, probably not. Everyone at home is well. But
some new information came to light shortly after you left,
and I thought you needed to know about it.' His gaze
strayed to Wyr.

'Can you bottle him up?' I said to Em.

'Gladly.'

'Wait—' said Wyr, then clapped his hands to his ears and
made a disgusted face. 'DEAF?' he thundered. 'GREAT.
THANKS.'

'It was that or an incomprehension charm,' said Em
with a faint smile. 'Perhaps he'd prefer to hear everything
in Swahili.'

'I like this approach,' I said. 'Simple. Effective.'

Em inclined her head.

'Can we leave it on him all the time?'

'I'm afraid not.'

'Muting charm?'

'No.'

'Damn.'

'Though I quite see the appeal.'

We all looked expectantly at Alban.

'It's two things,' he said, shaking his head as though to clear it. 'Firstly, Mother accelerated the translation process on Torvaston's papers. She seconded half a dozen language scholars from anywhere she could get them. Certain research projects at the University have ground to a halt, but we got the document finished. Did you know — or guess — that Torvaston had made *himself* into a kind of human griffin?'

I blinked. 'A what?'

'I don't mean half bird, or something like that. I'm not expressing this well.'

Small wonder, if he'd been criss-crossing back and forth between henge complexes for twelve hours straight. Or more. My unease grew. 'Carry on.'

'It's more the way griffins operate, in the magickal sense. You know, how they function as a source of magick, increase its potency in areas they populate, that kind of thing.'

'Got it. So Torvaston was doing the same thing?'

'Not just Torvaston. Do you remember that odd kind of... ritual you read about, at Farringale? From the diary? Where members of the Court went up to the top of the peak and, um, absorbed some of the griffins' excess magick.'

'Yes.'

'They were doing that to try to curb the overflow, or so we suppose, and that's probably true, but did you consider the probable long-term effects of that?'

'Sort of—'

'Or *how* it was done?'

'Sort of,' I said again. 'It's all been speculation.'

'Well, they had… tools, whether they knew it or not. A certain kind of metal — we don't know what it was, except that it was called *magickal silver* by Torvaston in his book — has a property which permits it to soak up magick like a sponge. And that happened to be a fashionable material at the Court of Farringale. Everyone who was anyone had at least a trinket made from the stuff.'

'Go on.'

'There's no known source of that metal anymore, and most examples of objects made from the stuff have passed out of existence or knowledge. Most.' He looked at me.

I had no trouble seeing where this was going. 'So they absorbed… too much magick,' I said faintly.

He shrugged. 'Maybe. Whatever the cause, the general effect the griffins had on Farringale spread to many members of the Court, too. Which was like… quadrupling the griffin population of Farringale in the space of a number of years. You can imagine the outcome.'

'That's how Farringale was flooded?'

'Probably. Torvaston's notes stop before the crisis, so we can't be sure, but the pieces fit.'

I felt saddened, somewhere under my unease. Torvaston's desperate attempts to mend Farringale had most likely contributed to its demise. We'd speculated about just such a possibility, but I was sorry to have it largely confirmed.

'But,' said Jay. 'But. What did they imagine they were doing with the excess magick? Absorbing it, however it was done, doesn't just make it go away.'

He was looking at me as he said that last part, and indeed I was functioning as living proof of that concept.

'Indeed not,' said Alban. 'Torvaston had a dual problem on his hands. He could see that Farringale was in danger of magickal excess — but he also had, we think, a touch of clairvoyance about him. His notes refer, more than once, to a "decline" he foresaw happening somewhere in the future. It seems he was attempting to manage a project which would solve both problems at once—'

'Oh,' I said. 'Somehow using the dangerously excessive magick of Farringale to balance out the decline that was beginning elsewhere?'

'Something like that,' Alban agreed. 'He began buying up all this *magickal silver* he could get his hands on. Almost bankrupted the royal family to do it, too. And he drew in all the brightest magickal minds he could get hold of in an attempt to build… some kind of device.'

'A device?'

'See, the problem with the flows of magick being under the influence of living creatures is that they can't be… managed, very well. They breed too much, or they die off, and disasters happen. Either the enclave is flooded out, or its magick dries up and the place just dies. Torvaston wanted a solution that could be carefully maintained, and that meant a non-biological one.'

Jay said, 'So he was building a… regulator.'

'Right.'

'Out of moonsilver. Or skysilver, or whatever the Yllanfalen call it.'

Alban looked oddly at him. 'You guessed that part.'

Jay just looked meaningfully at me.

'I was hoping,' said Alban, 'that the lyre hadn't—'

'It has,' I said. 'I used it. I'm sorry.'

He looked me over, more carefully, and I felt the faint brush of his magick against mine. 'Then I am too late,' he said heavily.

'Hey,' I said, trying for brightness. 'I'm still alive.'

'It's not that it's deadly,' said Alban, with a smile probably meant to be reassuring. 'Just… difficult to manage. Or reverse.'

'It does have its drawbacks,' I said lightly.

'And that's probably why the whole lot of them fled over here,' he continued. 'They would have felt less painfully overwrought, in a more potently magickal landscape. And they would have been less of a danger themselves. This is why they didn't join Her Majesty at Mandridore.'

And I sighed. If I'd hoped Alban would have some solution that said, *You CAN go home, Ves!* I was doomed to disappointment. 'Why didn't they throw away that damned *magickal silver*,' I said, somewhat sourly.

He smiled at me. 'Have you thrown away that lyre?'

'Fair point.'

'Magick has ever been seductive. Anything that can promise to amplify its potency, very much so.'

I couldn't disagree. 'And there's the whole question of dependency.'

'True.'

Which, secretly, bothered me the most. Swimming as I was in magick up to my very eyeballs, would it even be possible to go back to the way I was before? Would I... miss it? Would I *need* it? Had I, in fact, been turned into a raging magickal alcoholic overnight?

It didn't bear thinking about. Because I had a horrible feeling that I *would*.

'Okay, anyway,' I said briskly, setting these unproductive ideas aside. 'Do we know what became of Torvaston's magickal regulator?'

'Not exactly,' said Alban. 'We don't know if the project succeeded. If it did... the thing might still be at the old court, of course, but then presumably the disaster there would never have happened.'

'Baroness Tremayne would surely have said something about that, if it was,' I said. 'If she knew about it.'

'She probably didn't. Torvaston seems to have kept that particular project quiet, hence spending his family's money on it instead of the Court's.'

'Would he have left it behind?' said Jay.

'That's the thing we were thinking,' said Alban, shaking his head. 'If he had to leave our Britain, it seems far-fetched to imagine he'd abandon his life's work. And where better to complete so ambitious a project, but here?'

'Ohh,' I said, and stood straighter, electrified. 'It's *here*.'

'Specifically, probably, somewhere in those very mountains you're looking for,' said Alban. 'If it wasn't in Vale.'

'How do you know we already went to Vale?'

He grinned. 'Because I went up there first. Something about the trail of disaster and chaos I found struck me as very Ves-like.'

I blushed. 'It was necessary.'

'It always is.'

'So we're looking for Torvaston's masterpiece,' I said hurriedly. 'A thing which, if it had ever worked, could've saved Farringale.'

'And which *could* save countless other enclaves,' said Alban. 'Both those over-flooded with magick, and those starving to death without it.'

My eyes widened. 'This is big.'

'Very. And there's one more thing.'

'What's that?'

'You aren't the only ones.'

'What?'

Almost imperceptibly, he winced. 'That's the other thing I needed to tell you. There was a... spy uncovered, at Mandridore.'

'Uh oh.'

'Um, more than one. We've reason to think somebody gained access to these papers some time ago, may have had opportunity to translate at least parts of it. And someone, probably the same someone, had been trying very hard to get their hands on that scroll-case from Farringale.'

'Let me guess,' I said, with sinking heart. 'Someone with ties to Ancestria Magicka.'

'Bingo. And, Ves, I think they're already here.'

Of course they were. It was the answer to every question I'd ever asked myself about Fenella Beaumont's motives, or Ancestria Magicka's aims.

The mere thought of such an artefact falling into *those* hands brought me out into a cold sweat.

And they were, once again, way ahead of us.

'Giddy gods,' I said faintly. 'We're doomed.'

4

FOLLOWING ALBAN'S SEVERAL SHOCKING disclosures, an appalled silence fell. I wrestled with a growing sense of panic, and more or less succeeded in stuffing it back down. *Worst time in the history of magick to panic, Ves.*

Jay shook himself. 'Plan?' he said. 'We need a plan.'

'I suppose the plan's unchanged,' I said, watching Wyr with narrowed eyes. Something about him didn't seem quite right... 'I mean, we still need to get into Torvaston's secret mountain enclave.'

'Right,' said Jay.

'Just with a bit more urgency than before... you aren't actually deaf, are you?' I said, the latter directed at Wyr, who lay prone on the floor. His air of casual ease *had* seemed a bit studied.

He rolled his eyes and sat up. 'She's good,' he said, indicating Emellana with a nod of his head. 'But so am I.'

'So you heard all of that.'

'A fair bit of it, yes.'

'I've a theory,' I said. 'Let's test it.'

Wyr waited.

'*Ancestria Magicka.*'

Wyr sat like a stone, carefully failing to react.

'Last time I said that, you twitched.'

'Doubtful.'

'You did.'

'Did not.'

'*Can't* I just wring his neck?' I said plaintively, to no one in particular.

'No,' said Jay.

'Damnit.'

'But I might.'

Wyr held up his hands, and scooted back a bit. 'I deny everything.'

'He's heard of Ancestria Magicka, I'm sure of it,' I said, ignoring Wyr. 'How do you suppose that's possible?'

'He's met them before,' said Jay.

'Right. It's no coincidence that we ran into you, is it?' I nudged Wyr with my foot, a gesture not quite a kick. 'You were meant to intercept us.'

'Nope,' said Wyr.

With a sudden, swift movement, Emellana did exactly what I'd been dying to do. She swept the stupid hat off his head, and hurled it out over the peak. The wind caught it, and sent it sailing merrily away.

'Hey—' said Wyr.

He got no further, for Emellana picked *him* up, and stood poised to send him sailing straight after his hat. 'Still no?' she said in a pleasant tone.

Wyr swallowed. Good he might be, but I'd love to see the levitation charm that could contend with a precipitate fall down about a thousand feet. 'Er,' he said. 'Okay, I might have heard of them.'

'They hired you,' said Em.

'Maybe.'

'What were you supposed to do?'

Wyr sighed, hanging in Emellana's uncompromising grip like a sack of bricks. 'I was meant to help you.'

'*Help* us?' I said, frowning. 'Why? Oh.' I scrubbed at my face, frustrated with myself. 'They wanted the scroll-case.'

Wyr smiled nastily. 'It was good of you to make it so easy for me.'

'And Addie?'

'The unicorn? Anything else I could get off you I could keep. That was the deal.'

'Except the scroll-case?' I growled. 'Did you hand that over, or did you keep it?'

Wyr opened his mouth, and shut it again.

I found that Emellana was looking gravely at me. 'You've an idea?' I said to her.

'I think it is a good thing that Wyr has crossed our path again.'

I blinked. 'It is?'

'For one thing, it seems clear that the scroll-case may be important. If Mr. Wyr no longer has it, he is one of the few people who knows where it is.'

'All right.'

'He may also be one of the few people who knows where Torvaston's hideaway is to be found.'

'How do you figure that?'

'Why were you hired?' she said to Wyr. 'You're some kind of treasure hunter, aren't you?'

'It's a nicer name than "thief", I'll give you that,' said Wyr.

'You know all the old stories, especially those pertaining to ancient magick and potent artefacts. And you've made it your life's business to track them down. You're clearly on the best of terms with the traders up at Vale.'

'What's your point?' said Wyr.

'You know where Torvaston's hideaway is because you've been there. Ancestria Magicka probably hired you for that very purpose.'

Wyr examined his fingernails. 'I hate to contradict you when you're being so charmingly complimentary, but you're giving me too much credit. I haven't been in there, because no one has.'

'No one?'

'No. The *entrance* is known, but what's behind it remains a mystery because no one can open the damned door. Believe me. I've tried.'

'The scroll-case,' I said. 'Is that why you wanted it?'

'I don't imagine you noticed,' said Wyr, 'because it's faded, and camouflaged to boot. But there's a mark on that map just about exactly where the entrance is. Coincidence? I think not.'

'So you think something about the scroll-case either opens the door, or could explain how.'

'We're hoping so.'

By "we", I supposed he meant his crummy employers, too.

But.

'The case itself?' I said. 'Or something, perhaps, that was in it.'

I had the satisfaction of having, finally, disconcerted Wyr. 'There was something in it?' he said, looking in disbelief at me.

'When we found it, yes.'

'And you did what with the contents, exactly?'

'That would be my business.' I looked at the Baron. Hopefully my eyes said: *Tell me you brought the fork, the watch and the snuff box.*

Hopefully his smile said, *Of course I did.*

For once, Wyr appeared to have nothing to say.

I smiled. If he'd trotted off to Fenella Sodding Beaumont with that scroll-case and imagined he'd solved the mystery, he was in for a disappointment. They all were.

Provided, of course, that I was right, and it wasn't the case itself that held the secret.

Was it madness to gamble the entire success of our mission on the probability that a silver fork, a gilded pocket-watch and a questionably-decorated snuff box held the key to a lost enclave that generations had failed to penetrate?

Yes.

But madness is kind of my style.

'Well,' I said to Wyr. 'You'd better throw in your lot with us.'

'What?' said Jay.

'Why?' said Wyr.

'Because that case isn't going to get either you or Ancestria Magicka very far without its contents. And that means we've a much better chance of getting in than any of the rest of you.'

'Therefore?'

'Therefore, showing *us* the door is likely to work out better for your greedy little dreams.'

'Right,' said Wyr. 'You're just going to turn me loose in there and let me grab whatever I want. Sure.'

'There's one thing in there that we want. I don't think we need to care too much about the rest. Anything merely materially valuable is yours.' If we didn't manage to put a sock in him somewhere between here and the other side of that long-sealed door, anyway. I didn't give a crap about jewels and courtly goblets and what the hell else. I just wanted Torvaston's failed moonsilver project, and the books.

'Ves...' said Miranda, doubtfully.

'Got a better idea?'

She hesitated. 'No.'

'Me neither.'

Nor did anyone else, judging from the silence. Alban, to my delight, exuded a serene confidence in my judgement that I found highly gratifying.

I hoped it wasn't just a pretence.

'You're on,' said Wyr at last, and held out his hand to me.

I crossed to where he still dangled in Emellana's grip, and shook it. 'One thing,' I said. 'If you screw us over again, Emellana and the Baron will have you for dinner.'

'We like meat,' Alban offered, with a friendly smile.

Wyr gave him a sour look. 'Got it.'

Emellana didn't so much set him down as drop him from a great height.

'Ouch,' said Wyr, and picked himself up. 'Thanks for that.'

'Just deserts,' said Em.

I *did* so like her style.

Jay sidled my way. 'Where did all that come from?' he said in an undertone.

'About the contents of the case?' I whispered back. 'Do you recall much about the history of table etiquette?'

'Not... really.'

'I was forgetting it myself, until just now. See, we saw a metal utensil with a handle and twin prongs and immediately connected it with tableware. And it *does* resemble an early fork. But the fork didn't come into common use in western Europe until the eighteenth century, and this thing has to be like a century and a half older than that.'

'It isn't a fork!'

'Exactly. Also, the pocket-watch isn't so badly out of place, except that it has two hands. Early ones had only an hour hand.'

'So it... isn't telling the time?'

'Might be. Might be tracking something else entirely.'

'And the box?'

I shrugged. 'Snuff was coming into fashion by the early sixteen hundreds, so it could just be a snuff box. Then again, maybe not. And there's no saying that it was used to *hold* snuff, even if it is.'

Jay grinned. 'Who knew a taste for historical trivia could be so useful.'

'Well, me. It's not like it's the first time.'

'The secret of your success?'

I thought about that. 'Yes,' I decided. 'It pretty much is.'

5

'YOU KNOW HE'S GOING to mess us up first chance he gets?' said Jay, eyeing Wyr sourly. The subject of his justifiable resentment was still in Emellana's custody, engaged in some loud debate I had not bothered to listen to. But as I watched, Emellana released him — none too gently — and his gaze fastened instantly on Jay and I, obviously holding secret counsels without him.

'I know,' I murmured. 'I'm counting on it.'

'Wha—' said Jay.

Slightly louder, I said: 'I know, Jay, and you're right to be concerned. Just don't tell him about the Wand and the ring, all right? It's best if he doesn't know what was in that scroll-case.'

Jay, to his credit, only blinked once at me in confusion before his face cleared to impassiveness, and he nodded.

His eyes shifted sideways to Wyr in a creditable display of craftiness.

Wyr gave no sign of having heard me. 'Ready to go?' he said, and I noticed he gave Baron Alban a wide berth as he passed.

'Quickly, please.'

Miranda, to my surprise, spoke up. 'One question, first. Whereabouts did you leave your new employers, Wyr?'

'Lady Fenella? Truth be told, I haven't seen her in a while.'

I thought I saw relief on Miranda's face, before she turned away. No wonder. She'd defected to Fenella Beaumont's miserable organisation, only to (hopefully) defect back; she wasn't going to be popular with anybody, at this rate.

Course, one could rely on nothing Wyr said. Me, I counted on running into a few of our least favourite foes the moment we got anywhere near Torvaston's Enclave.

Couldn't be helped.

'Tokens?' said Wyr.

I'd noticed Alban stuffing handfuls of the things into his pockets soon after he had appeared, but those would doubtless be to whichever henges he'd yet to go in search of us. Not much use. 'We will be travelling with Patel Windways,' I said.

Wyr looked nonplussed.

'That guy,' I clarified, pointing at Jay.

'You know that's—'

'Illegal,' I said, interrupting him. 'We know.'

'You'll be thieving in no time.'

I opened my mouth to object to this monstrously unfair charge, but had to close it again in silence. Not only had I given the sneak permission to plunder Torvaston's Enclave at his leisure, I also proposed to divest the place of its most important and valuable artefact myself. We could argue semantics and historical-rights-of-ownership all day, and it would still all boil down to something uncomfortably close to theft.

Noticing he had successfully got under my skin, Wyr grinned at me. 'Well, ladies and gents, we're heading north,' he said. 'Far north.'

I wasted a moment in useless doubts. He *was* a back-stabbing little shit. Would even the promise of un-contested plunder of a lost king's personal effects be enough to keep him in line? Was he taking us to the Hyn-dorin Mountains, or was he once again sweeping us away to somewhere else?

I shook the thoughts away. It was a gamble worth taking. The worst he could do was delay us (again); meanwhile, it could take us days or weeks to work out where to go without help.

'Lead on,' I said. 'We're right behind you.'

THAT HE HAD INDEED taken us far north seemed indubitable, a half-hour or so later. We exited the last of a sequence of henge-complexes, each decreasing in size, upon a windy peak somewhere bone-chillingly cold. Also distressingly short on oxygen.

Maybe this was the brilliant new plan. Drop us somewhere freezing and dangerously high up, and leave us to die of exposure.

No, he couldn't do that. The way out was embedded into the rock, a circle of weathered, craggy stones swept clean by the wind. The landscape offered little else in the way of hope. We stood, miserably huddled, on a soaring mountainside, surrounded by nothing but more mountains. Bleak and beautiful, these peaks were of a deep, dark stone; snow dusted the tops of those on the near horizon, rising still higher into the mist-white skies.

'This way,' said Wyr, and set off, winding his way in between two jutting crags. He had his hands in his pockets, probably to protect them from the cold, but he seemed untouched by the conditions. He sauntered off, whistling.

'Your ring is gone,' said Alban in my ear.

That cost me a pang. Yes, I had deliberately hung it out as bait for the double-crossing thief. No, I didn't love losing it.

'Then I guess I'm stuck with pink hair forever,' I said.

'Luckily, it suits you.'

I smiled up at him. 'You can definitely stay.'

'That was the plan.'

We set off after Wyr, me keeping a weather eye on the horizon for any unhappy surprises leaping out of the air. I trusted Jay to keep track of where we were going, in case we needed to find our way back to the henge. 'You *do* have the mysterious miscellany somewhere about your person?' I said softly to Alban.

'You mean the other... articles? Yes, I do.'

'Thank goodness.'

He grinned. 'Your faith in me is touching.'

'Actually I had no idea if you'd thought to bring them along.'

'...that was a gamble?'

'Yep.'

'You're a brave woman.'

'Or stark raving mad. The point is the subject of some debate, at Home.'

'Fair.'

'I don't know why I didn't think of it before we left.'

'Other things on your mind.'

True, but that was little excuse. I suppose the peculiar paraphernalia had seemed so random as to be hardly relevant, and I hadn't set eyes on any of it since that last trip to Mandridore. I'd clean forgotten.

Fortunate that we had Alban to rectify that particular mistake.

Then again, if I had brought them with me, they would probably have disappeared into Wyr's possession along with the scroll-case. Swings and roundabouts.

Wyr led us on a winding route, bearing steadily downwards towards a sloping valley below. We walked for the best part of half an hour, getting colder by the minute. By the time he finally stopped, my teeth were chattering. Even Alban looked uncomfortable.

'And here,' said Wyr, 'is where we all part ways with the straight and narrow.' He gestured at the ground, his hand tracing a vaguely circular shape in the air.

Without which clue, I might never have spotted the henge. It was so deeply embedded as to be virtually invisible, only the rough outlines of a ring of rock discernible. 'More Ways?' I said.

'This one isn't part of the official network, and you can't buy tokens to use it.'

'How did *you* know about it?' said Jay. I saw his point. The stone circle was so well camouflaged, if I hadn't known what I was looking for, I'd never have spotted it at all.

'Old diaries, old stories, rumours and whispers and many, many weeks of searching,' said Wyr. 'None of which,' he added with a twisted smile, 'were conducted by me. I just bought the information.'

'Nice when you can get away with that,' said Jay sourly.

'Extremely. Shall we go?'

Jay looked drawn and tired, and small wonder; we had worked him pretty hard even to get this far. But he was growing accustomed to the potency of the Ways out here, or so I assumed, for while he looked weary, he also looked composed. Sane. Not losing his marbles, as he had the first time he had travelled by henge complex.

Still, I felt a flicker of concern for him. 'Are there many more?' I asked of Wyr.

'This is the last one.'

I looked questioningly at Jay, who nodded back. *I'm fine*, that meant.

Whether he was genuinely fine or just being a raging man about everything, who was to say? We didn't have a lot of choice but to let him take us through.

'I'm going first, with Ves and Alban,' Jay announced.

Was he too tired to take all of us at once, or was this a precaution? I couldn't read his expression. 'Fine,' I said, and stepped up to his side.

Alban joined us on Jay's other side, and Jay began the process of summoning the Winds of the Ways. A swift breeze swept up, and blew back my hair. It smelled, oddly, of cherries.

'Where does this one go to?' I said to Wyr.

'Into the Hyndorin Enclave.'

'What? I thought you said it had been closed for centuries.'

'Not the entire thing. Just the part that matters, that being wherever Torvaston and his friends settled.'

I wanted to ask more questions, specifically about what there was to expect in the mythical Hyndorin hideaway. But I was too late. In a whirl of Winds and a flurry of snowflakes — somehow — Jay swept us away.

And in that instant, Wyr made a lunge for us. I felt him fall heavily against my side — the side upon which my trusty satchel hung — and he clung to me as we travelled through the Ways.

When the whirl of motion ceased and the world stopped spinning around us, I opened my eyes to the sight of Wyr sprinting away from us.

Mellow sunlight glinted off the shape of my beloved Sunstone Wand, clutched tight in his hand.

'Well,' I said. 'That got rid of him.'

Jay pressed my hand in brief sympathy. I suppose he knew what it cost me to turn those two treasures over to Wyr, and watch him abscond with them.

I reminded myself that retrieving them was not beyond the bounds of possibility, and that even if it was, they were well lost. This time, Wyr had played right into *my* hands, and I intended to capitalise on that.

'We need to follow him,' I said. 'Quickly. He's on his way to Torvaston's doorstep, or my name isn't Ves.'

'Right.' Jay gathered himself, and vanished.

'Your name isn't Ves,' said Alban. 'Technically.'

'And you aren't technically a baron.'

'Touché.'

We had ended up somewhere I never could have expected. Considering everything — like the references to the Hyndorin *Mountains,* for one, and Torvaston's hand-drawn map suggestive of rugged peaks — I had anticipated a properly mountainous landscape. Actually, we were in a green-and-golden valley, apparently in the height of summer. Tufts of feathery, heathery purple were dotted here and there, together with sufficient flowers to drown in. And while I am something of an enthusiast for flowers, I recognised exactly none of the species I saw around me.

Trees we had, too, the gnarly kind indicative of great age. Despite this, they were laden with blossom and swelling fruits — including something that smelled like cherries, even if they looked more like apples. That explained that aroma.

Meanwhile, despite the evidence of high summer going on all around us, the skies overhead were as misty-white as those above the peaks we'd just come through. And, most peculiarly of all, a light dusting of snow drifted steadily down from those skies, though it vanished or melted away before it could reach so much as a single blade of the grass upon the ground.

The flow of magick was significantly more potent. Not Vale levels, not yet. Chaotic enough to produce some odd and interesting effects, though. Strong enough to ease the skin-prickling discomfort and head-swimming disorientation I'd suffered ever since we had left the vicinity of Vale.

I liked it at once.

'Strangest Enclave yet, by a mile,' I said, keeping an eye on the direction Wyr had gone in. He was rapidly vanishing from sight. I wanted to hare madly after him, before he could disappear altogether into the mist.

But I also didn't want to do this without Jay, and Em, and Miranda.

'I've never even heard of—' said Alban, holding out a hand to catch a bit of the uncanny snow.

But as he spoke, a gaggle of people exploded into the waiting henge: Jay, Em, and Miranda, with Pup struggling in Emellana's arms.

'Everyone okay?' I said, looking especially at Jay.

Too out of breath to speak, he nonetheless managed a nod in answer to my question. I wished we had time to let him rest, but we didn't.

'Righto,' I said. 'Mir, can you send up your bird? We need to track Wyr.'

'Done.' Miranda gave a soft whistle, and something small shot up into the air in a blur of bright blue feathers.

I retrieved Pup from Emellana's grip, and set her down. 'Pup of mine,' I said. 'It's your turn to save the day. Remember Wyr?'

Pup sat staring up at me, grinning and wagging her tufty yellow tail. A single snowflake settled on the tip of her stubby horn.

'If you can catch him, you can bite him,' I said, and pointed.

Pup gave a series of yaps, turned in a frenzied circle, and then tore off after Wyr.

'And now we run,' I said, praying for a burst of unnatural speed courtesy of my unnaturally magickal state.

Taking a deep, deep breath, I legged it after the Pup — and Wyr.

6

I TORE THROUGH THE unnatural mountain valley on the trail of Wyr, my Pup, and the long-sealed door to Torvaston's settlement. Whether the gods had answered my hasty prayers and granted me a burst of speed, or whether my magickally supercharged state put wings to my feet, I began to gain on Wyr despite his head start. He charged headlong through the verdant grasses like a fox with a pack of hounds on his tail; that, I supposed, made me the hounds. I could be sorely tempted to tear him apart with my teeth, too, once I caught him — if Pup didn't beat me to it. I didn't *think* she had too many violent tendencies, but one never knew. Wyr could rouse the bloodthirsty instincts of a block of stone.

It occurred to me, as I pelted along, to wonder where Wyr thought he was going. His flight seemed aimless;

around us and ahead of us stretched the same, unbroken grassy landscape, dotted with the same patches of purple heather, the same wizened old trees. No apparent destination rose upon the horizon, nowhere for a fleeing thief to take refuge. Nowhere for a legendary door to lie hidden, either.

I was forgetting the unusual behaviour of mountains, in Enclaves associated with that ancient troll court. Between one step and the next, the mists cleared from the skies; looming with shocking suddenness out of the ether rose a peak the equal of its majestic twin at old Farringale.

Complete with its own complement of griffin residents. Enormous nests were dotted here and there up the rocky face of the mountain — apparently unscaleable, considering its absolutely sheer sides — and in the far distance, I glimpsed a few familiar, dark, winged shapes wheeling upon the winds.

I felt a moment's strong satisfaction. Hadn't we said there would be griffins here? The pleasure of having a theory confirmed never gets old, however many times one is proved deliciously, perfectly correct.

But that was to grow distracted from the point, because I was still hurtling towards a sheer rock face at improbable speed, and so were Wyr and my absurd, furiously yapping pup. Something about the shape and structure of that peak struck me as odd; *too* structured, too symmetrical, too sheer. Not altogether natural.

I didn't have time to study it any more closely. Ahead of me, Wyr skidded to a stop at the base of the peak, and stared — hopelessly? — up at the unclimbable expanse of rock before him.

'Wyr!' I yelled. 'Giddy gods, where is the damned *door.*'

He did not look back. I forced air into my burning lungs and energy into my flagging legs, and put on a final burst of speed in a bid to catch up. Not that he had anywhere to go—

—I stopped dead as Wyr shot skywards, borne by a slab of levitating rock which had, to my eye, come out of nowhere. He'd stepped onto it deliberately, of course, though by what mechanism he'd caused the thing to bear him up the peak I couldn't tell. Perhaps he hadn't. Perhaps it did that by itself.

Stranger things were happening out here.

Unfortunately, that was the very same moment that Pup caught up with him. Fastening her sharp little teeth into his leg with a yip of victory, she, too, was borne haplessly upwards, attached to his trouser-leg.

'Pup!' I wailed.

Wyr's involuntary cry of pain was my only consolation.

I paused a moment in frozen dismay. Wyr had out-jock-eyed us *again*, and this time we'd lost poor Pup to his wiles as well.

I shook myself. *Get a grip, Ves.* If there was one unusually buoyant slab of stone attached to this peculiar peak, there could well be more.

Alban, Jay and the others found me there some minutes later, urgently questing for a second magickal elevator and coming up with nothing.

'Was that a scrap of yellow fur I saw hurtling up the peak a minute ago?' panted Jay, coming to a stop near me.

'A scrap of bitey, yappy yellow fur, which has yet to come down,' I replied. 'Help me.'

'With?'

'Wyr, the Pup and presumably the door are somewhere up there, and we are not.' I'd walked back and forth and around and back and forth and around and found noth-ing useful, and was rapidly growing desperate. We were *so close.*

'He's not that far up, Ves,' said Miranda, and I belatedly remembered the lirrabird she'd sent up to keep an eye on Wyr. She pointed upwards. 'Maybe fifty, sixty feet?'

I stared up in the direction of her pointing finger, with-out much effect. Thick, swirling mist obscured my view.

Right.

There comes a time in every adventure when you have to check in with yourself and find out how crazy you're feeling.

Is it important enough?

Yes.

Are you brave enough?

Hell, yes.

'Forget it,' I said, calling off the pointless search. 'Just find me a slab of stone. Couple of feet wide, not too heavy.'

Alban and Jay gave me identical, doubting looks. 'You're not thinking what I think you're thinking?' Jay said.

'Ves, I know you're fond of Goodie but let's not be completely insane,' said Alban.

I shot both of them a look that said, *Have we* met *before?* 'The stone?' I said.

It was Emellana who found it: a neatish disk of stone, a few inches thick and just wide enough for me to fit both feet onto it. 'You rock,' I informed her, taking it. 'Again. Thank you.'

She gave me her faint, amused smile. 'Be careful up there.'

I dropped the stone and stepped onto it, spared a futile wish that it hadn't been necessary to sacrifice my Sunstone Wand, and delivered a bolt of pure magick to the hapless stone beneath my feet.

'Ves, sixty feet up is *pretty damned far*,' I heard Jay yell as I shot into the skies.

See, levitating isn't usually my strong point. I'm lucky if I can manage more than a few feet.

But I'd be damned if I wasn't going to get some *use* out of my inconveniently magick-drenched state. A feeling of dreamy serenity had been growing upon me ever since I had set foot in Torvaston's enclave, that itchy, *wrong* feeling draining away entirely. I hoped that meant that my surroundings and I were nicely balanced, or something nearer to it. I hoped that meant that me and my overflowing magicks could do mad, wonderful things together.

I shoved everything I had at that slip of stone, and catapulted myself upwards at what felt like fifty miles an hour.

If a thin, idiotic shriek was heard to reverberate around that peak at that moment, I confess it was me.

Up sixty feet I went, and more. And *more*. Frantic, I tried to turn off that insane flow of magick. *Like it has a tap or something,* I thought disgustedly, succeeding only in slowing my pace. *Nice one, Ves.* At this rate I'd hit the top of the peak in no time, making of myself a tasty griffin-snack.

Or I'd just fall off the damned stone, and plummet to a grisly death below. *Not in front of Alban*, I thought absurdly, and a hysterical giggle tore itself from my throat. Holding myself steady on the stone was taking too much effort; the higher I went, the more powerful the winds that sought to knock me clean off my perch.

Right. *Stop dithering.* Gritting my teeth, I held grimly to position atop the stone, tried not to notice the way I'd begun to spin like a sodding top, and reversed the flow of magick. Instead of boosting me up, I wanted it pushing me *down.*

My headlong pace slowed, and slowed further. Heart hammering, I kept my eyes turned resolutely away from everything that rose above and — oh no, not below, don't look *down,* you utter fool, could you be any more *stupid—*

The one good thing about being two hundred feet up (or more)? There's no one up there to hear you scream.

Dignity intact.

Sort of.

But at last, to my weak-kneed relief, I ceased shooting up higher, and began to sink.

Carefully, I admonished myself. *How about we don't do this at a potentially fatal pace?*

Down, down we went, and human magickal battery or no, it was the hardest thing I have ever done, no contest. Later, I'd look back on that scintillating three minutes of my life and wonder what in the giddy gods was *wrong with me.*

'Batshit crazy, Ves,' I said out loud as I swooped back down the peak. 'You might want to work on that.'

There: a tuft of bright yellow, not far below. I squinted, and as I sank several more feet through the drifting white mists I detected a plateau upon the mountainside, atop which stood Wyr, and Pup. As I drew closer — flying my stone contraption like a pro by then, if I do say so myself — I saw something else, something that made my overcharged heart beat faster with excitement rather than terror.

An enormous stone door was set into the rock. Made from a single, huge, carved slab, it had the weathered look of great age. It was smooth and unmarked, which I thought was unfair. If this was the Lord of the Rings, there'd be a convenient runic inscription offering us the password.

'Hi,' I said as my stone plinth came to rest atop the plateau.

Wyr did a proper double-take, and stared at me in utter disbelief. Was there even a tinge of awe? 'You cannot be serious,' he said. '*How?*'

'I'm temporarily possessed of godlike magickal powers,' I said, with all the nonchalance I could muster. Never mind that my knees were shaking, my legs felt like jelly, and I had a strong desire to collapse all over the blessedly solid rock beneath my feet and cover it with kisses.

Instead, I scooped up my pup. She had abandoned her assault on Wyr's leg by then, and sat cheerfully watching his total lack of progress with the door, a scrap of his trouser-leg still stuck in her teeth.

Wyr's leg was bleeding, to my satisfaction. *Petty, Ves,* I chided myself, but it didn't help.

'Any luck?' I said, rewarding lovely, bloodthirsty Goodie with a thorough cuddle.

He had my Sunstone Wand and my ring in one hand, and the scroll-case in the other. What he'd been trying to do with them that might have the power to open the door, I couldn't say.

'Not yet,' he said, eyeing me warily.

Did he think I was going to try to retrieve them? I was tempted, but they were keeping him busy and that was more important just then.

Pup watched the Wand's progress with greedy avarice.

I knew how she felt.

'Be right back,' I said, and stepped onto the slab of stone by which Wyr had travelled up to the door. As I'd hoped, the moment I rested my weight upon it, it began to move, and sailed smoothly back down.

I left Wyr gazing after me, nonplussed.

At ground level, I was greeted by four wide-eyed, possibly angry people. Or three such people, and Emellana.

'Impressive,' said she, unruffled as ever.

'Thanks.' I held out my fist for a bump, which she bestowed. 'There's a door up there with an oddly-shaped keyhole.'

Nobody answered me.

'Alban?' I prompted. 'The fork? There are twin holes spaced about an inch apart, very small. The fork-thing should fit, I hope? I don't know if that's going to be enough by itself, or whether we'll need the watch or something as well—'

'I just had about eight heart attacks in quick succession,' said Jay.

'Me too,' said Alban.

'That makes three of us,' I said, attempting a smile.

I received only a flat stare in response, from Jay at least. Alban, though undoubtedly appalled, also regarded me with something like... admiration.

'Are you always this reckless?' he said, doing something quizzical with his eyebrows.

'Yes,' said Miranda. 'She's famous for it.'

I gave her the look of utter betrayal, which she waved away. 'Any other person would be thoroughly dead by now. Somehow, when it's Ves, she... pulls it off.'

'To say the least,' said Alban, with a flash of that grin I loved.

Not the time to get distracted, Ves.

'Can we talk about this later?' I said. 'We've a door to open and a thief to dispose of.'

Jay gave me a shocked look.

'Er, not fatally,' I clarified.

'Right.'

'Probably.'

Alban produced the not-fork, the possible-watch and the probably-snuff box from a pocket, and put them into my hands. I read a little reserve in his demeanour, and suffered a moment's remorse. He'd truly thought I was about to die. So had Jay.

To be fair, I might have.

I hardened my heart. *Needs must.* Hasn't that always been the way?

'Thank you,' I murmured.

He briefly squeezed my hand, and released it.

My heart eased a little.

'Right,' I said, stepping back onto the lift. 'Pile on. We're going up.'

Alban joined me, and Jay, and Em. There was just room enough for Miranda to join us, and the stone began to rise.

7

WE FOUND WYR FURIOUSLY waving my Sunstone Wand around: poking the door with its tip, trying to slot it into those twin keyholes I'd noticed, drawing invisible symbols over the stone surface, and occasionally shaking it in irritation. We watched this display in silence for a few seconds, with (at least on my part) great enjoyment.

'Hi!' I said after a moment.

Wyr jumped, and spun around. 'Damnit,' he growled. 'You can't have these back.' He stood braced, as though he would withstand our combined attack by force of will alone.

'All right,' I said mildly. For the moment at least, I did not seem to need them.

I tested this by flicking my fingers over my hair. Its pink hue did not fade, but it was joined by six or seven other shades, until I had a shimmering rainbow mane.

I gave this a casual toss, while I thought about what precisely to do to Wyr.

'Ves,' murmured Jay. 'I hate to be a downer, but I don't think a change of hair colour is going to help much here.'

'I'd think you would know better by now,' I said.

It took him a second to realise that I hadn't retrieved my colour-changing ring from Wyr's possession. It still adorned our unwilling comrade's thumb.

I caught the sideways glance he threw at me then, the narrowing of the eyes.

By then I had decided. 'This is nothing personal,' I said to Wyr. 'Or, not very much. But you're in the way.'

'Wait—' said Wyr, as I stretched out my hand.

Too late. An instant later, a small tree grew where Wyr had been standing. It only rose as high as my waist, but its slim branches were laden with the cherry-scented apples we had seen back down in the valley below.

'Hrm,' I said, frowning at it. 'I was going for pancakes.'

'You...' Jay said, before words apparently failed him. 'You've turned him into a tree.'

'It could at least have been a pancake tree,' I said, sadly. 'I need some practice.'

Jay took a big step back from me, holding up his hands in a gesture of surrender. 'Not on me!'

'No, that would be silly,' I agreed.

'*That* would be silly?' Jay yelped.

'Never underestimate a woman with rainbow hair,' murmured Alban.

'Noted,' said Jay.

I noticed something else. The smell of fresh cherries emanating from the Wyr-tree was creating a sensation I hadn't experienced since Vale: hunger.

I was *hungry* again!

And... and tired. Tired like a woman who had sat in a magick-warping chair all night while her companions slumbered around her, too wired to close her eyes.

Damnit. Poor timing.

'*Anyway*,' said Miranda. 'How long will he stay like that?'

I looked down at my handiwork. 'I have no idea.'

'Perhaps we'd better get on, then?'

'Right.' I held up my right hand, in which I wielded the double-pronged implement of (hopefully) opening, and intoned, 'Fork.' I turned to test my theory as to where it went.

'Ah,' I said. 'Alban. Perhaps you'd better do this part.' I handed him the fork.

Alban, troll-tall and able, therefore, to reach the keyhole, carefully inserted the fork-key into the twin holes. It slotted in easily, a perfect fit.

I waited, holding my breath, for the sounds of a lock clicking back, or hinges creaking as the door opened for us.

All I heard was Pup's whimper as she pawed at the Wyr-tree. I pretended not to notice when she squatted and, er, watered the base of its trunk.

'It doesn't turn or something?' I said to Alban.

He shook his head, and demonstrated its absolute immobility. 'It fits in there, but... that's all.'

I looked at Emellana. 'Any ideas?'

She considered the question in what I hoped was a promising silence, then said, 'No.'

I sighed. 'Anybody?'

'There *were* three things in that case,' Jay pointed out. 'Perhaps there's more to this than a weird key.'

I took out the watch. Being of troll craftsmanship, it was a lot bigger than most of the examples I had seen, and heavy. 'No tarnish,' I murmured, running my thumb over the gleaming, silvery metal. 'Has anyone cleaned this?'

'I don't know for certain,' said Alban. 'It hasn't been under my care.'

It had no glass, the mechanical parts instead protected by an ornately-patterned silver case. I opened it, and beheld a clock face made from something resembling ivory. I hoped it wasn't unicorn horn, but based on everything we had seen at Vale, I did not hold out much hope there. No numerals were etched into that circular face; instead, intervals were marked with tiny bubbles of coloured jewels embedded into the ivory/unicorn horn/whatever it was.

I counted. Nine, not twelve.

Also, a new detail I had failed to note before: it did not have two hands. It had three. One, perhaps, had been concealed behind another, the last time I had taken a brief glance at it. Now, all three were splayed out around the face, and none of them appeared to be moving.

'Not a clock,' I said, passing it to Emellana.

Jay was deep in study of the snuff box, with (slightly to my surprise) Miranda leaning over his shoulder. 'There's nothing in it?' she was saying.

Jay opened the lid to display its emptiness. 'It really looks like a snuff box, but—' he lifted it to his nose, and inhaled. 'It doesn't smell like it's ever held anything like snuff.'

'It's old,' Miranda pointed out. 'If it's been empty for a long time, there might not be any lingering smell.'

'Maybe,' Jay agreed. 'But snuff's pungent stuff, especially the flavoured blends. It does linger.'

'So you think it wasn't used to hold snuff?'

'I can't think of a reason why Torvaston would keep something so mundane in so important a scroll-case, alongside the key to *this* door,' said Jay. 'Can you?'

'No. So, what was it supposed to hold?'

'No clue.'

'Alban,' I said, sidling his way. 'There wasn't anything in the papers that might give us a hint?'

He shook his head. 'Torvaston never mentioned any of this.'

'He wouldn't, I suppose,' I said, remembering. 'The papers date from before the fall of Farringale, right?'

'Right.'

I sighed, disappointed. And stymied. The watch (or whatever it was) might be pretty, and intriguing, but to look at it was to receive no indication whatsoever of its function, and an empty box could be of no use at all.

'Ves,' said Emellana.

I looked up. 'Tell me you have something.'

She had walked away to the very edge of the plateau, and now walked back, holding the watch out in front of her. 'Walk with me.'

I obeyed, Alban falling in beside me. We paced from one side of the plateau to the other, eyes fixed upon the jewelled clock-face.

Almost imperceptibly, one of the three silver hands moved.

'I think,' said Emellana, 'that maybe it is not a watch, but more some kind of a... compass.'

'With three hands?' said Alban.

'Whatever it is attracted to is perhaps complicated.'

'Doubtless,' I said, excitement rising. 'Em, you might have cracked it!'

Emellana returned to the stone-slab of a lift, and stepped onto it. 'Let's go for a walk,' she said.

Ten minutes later, we made another discovery.

Following Em's lead, we wandered through the sun-lit valley, watching breathlessly as one or another of the three hands slowly moved around the compass's face. It wasn't just the hands that were affected by movement, either; while it was difficult to detect in the bright light of the morning, the jewels around the rim brightened and dimmed with a faint magickal glow. They were collected broadly into three colours, too: blue gems formed a row of three, followed by shades of green, and finally three purplish jewels. They tended to react in concert.

'Pick a colour,' I said after several minutes of tramping aimlessly about. 'Look. When the shortest hand moves, the blue ones shine. The green ones seem to respond to the middle hand, and the purple ones to the longest.'

'Purple,' said Em, and adjusted her direction. Instead of walking in circles, we walked until the longest of the three silver hands edged around the face, and kept to that direction. The compass led us back into the orchard of tangled trees, some distance from the mountain — which had, a glance back revealed, faded once again into the white mist.

Nothing emerged from the trees, nothing met my eyes that might explain why the compass had brought us tramping in this direction, and we were only getting farther from the door. My excitement began to ebb. What if neither the compass nor the box had anything to do with opening the way? Were we wasting time?

Emellana stopped, in between two withered old orchard trees. In the shadow cast by their arching boughs, the soft glow of the purple jewels appeared stronger.

Or maybe they shone brighter because we were onto something. The long hand had stopped in the dead centre of those three purplish gems, and as we watched, the glow grew brighter and deeper.

'Em,' I said in awe. 'You're purple.'

She glanced down at her amethyst-coloured shirt. 'I know.'

'No. I mean... you're *glowing.*' A swirl of something misty billowed up around Emellana, shimmering and purple, and soared into the sky.

I watched in silence as a trio of butterflies drifted into the whirl of light and hovered there, softly aglow.

'What happens if you step out?' said Jay.

Emellana took three big steps away, and the mist and lights promptly died away.

Alban took the compass from her. 'And back?' he said.

When Emellana returned to her former spot, the glow returned. What's more, it was definitely coming from *her*. Even her skin glimmered with that weird purple light.

'It seems I am stuck here,' she said, ruefully.

'We'll find the other two,' I said. 'And giddy gods, I hope this doesn't only work for trolls, or we're a team member short.'

Alban eyed the compass in his hands, and gave a tiny sigh. 'I perceive it is my fate to become a magickal beacon.'

'Only for a little while,' I promised, hoping I spoke the truth. 'Pick a colour.'

'Blue.'

'Be quick,' Em said. 'It is my belief that these points move around.'

'Why would they—' I began, and shut up. 'Of course. Why would there need to be a compass, if the beacon-points were fixed?'

'Precisely.'

We left Emellana standing in her whorl of magick, and followed the compass once more, moving rather faster than before. *Blue* turned out to live a few hundred feet away, in an open spot in the meadow. Alban lit up like a sapphire-coloured firework — not quite so explosively, thank goodness — and stood there, arms folded, as butterflies settled in his hair. 'Okay. And who's taking green?'

'It will have to be you or me,' Jay said to Miranda. 'Whatever's going on with Ves I don't know, but she seems to be the best person to head inside first.'

Was that a compliment, or was I being fed to the wolves? 'It could be dangerous,' I said to Jay, glowering.

'And you've just turned a person into a tree.'

'... good point.'

'You'll have one of us with you, too.'

I pick you, I thought, but did not say aloud.

Miranda, though, is not stupid. 'Fine,' she sighed, and held out her hand for the compass.

Alban gave it over. 'It tickles,' he informed her gravely.

'The light?'

Alban nodded once.

'Lucky that I'm not ticklish,' she said, marching off. 'Oh no wait, I *am*.'

I looked back once, in the direction we'd left Emellana. I could still see her flurry of purple mist and light, flowing into the skies. By now it was thick with butterflies and, doubtless, other wingy things.

I disliked having to leave three-fifths of my team behind in keeping the things activated, but if it had to be that way, then so be it.

I hoped, at least, that it would successfully open the door.

'Right,' said Miranda shortly afterwards, installed atop the half-rotten stump of a fallen tree, and lit up with verdant green. 'Please get on with it, before I drown in insects.'

A quick glance, to check. There was Em's beacon, still aglow, and Alban's column of blue. Miranda's gathered quickly in radiance, until it hurt to look at her.

'We'll be—' I said.

'*Ves.*' Jay hit my arm, and pointed.

'What— giddy *gods.*' The mountain was back. We were nowhere near it, but whatever enchantment had hidden it from a distance was visibly evaporating into nothing. The mountain loomed over the valley, glittering with snow and magick and — gods, the griffins. They were whirling up there, hundreds of them, and a whirl of coloured light — familiar colours, these, purple and green and blue — engulfed the whole lot.

I could just see the gigantic door as it... vanished. Indeed, half the rock-face disappeared.

'It's not a mountain,' I breathed. 'It's a *tower.*'

8

I STARED IN DISBELIEF at the stupendous tower looming out of the misty remnants of what had appeared to be an impregnable mountain. Absolutely *had* been, in fact; had I not stood upon it myself, not long ago? Had there not been a door set into its side? My mind reeled at the power and complexity of such an illusion. What had Torvaston wrought, out in the wilds of this wondrously magickal Britain?

And damn me if the entire thing wasn't built out of starstone, to boot. Like Melmidoc's spire. I couldn't be sure until twilight, of course, when it would most probably develop that distinctive blue glimmer. But the way the white stone shone pearly in the sun looked awfully familiar.

'Go,' Miranda said, shoving the compass into my hands.

I hesitated, looking at Pup, who was questing in circles around my feet. 'Will you look after—'

'Take her with you,' Miranda said. 'Never know what she'll find.'

How true that had repeatedly proved. 'Right,' I said. 'Follow when you can.'

I took off running, Jay pounding along at my heels. The tower was built upon a rocky promontory of considerable height; as we drew nearer, I saw that the stone "lift" was still there, still poised to ferry visitors up to the door some sixty feet above ground level. The structure was of an architectural style I had never before seen, and it's hard to coherently describe. The doors and windows were narrow and tall, with pointed arches; a little gothic, but bigger, archier, airier, and curlicued. The conical roof crowning the tower spread unusually wide, and ought to have been top heavy, but the effect was somehow graceful. As for the body of the tower, it had the look of a building that had once had straight walls — until someone impossibly large had taken hold of the top, and twisted it into an elegant spiral.

'I'd have thought it would resemble Farringale,' I said to Jay as we approached the lift, both our necks craning to keep the impossible tower in view.

'It resembles nothing I've ever seen,' he said, awed.

I gazed up and up as the lift carried us skywards. Far above, the griffins wheeled and turned around the pinnacle of the tower, just as though it were a mountain still. I braced myself as we neared the door, in case any of them should object to our approach. But they drifted on, serene and oblivious.

The Wyr-tree still stood at the top. I felt a moment's dismay upon beholding it, for though Wyr's continued disablement was mighty convenient, I began to wonder how long he would remain in the shape of a tree. The past day or so, it was like I'd been handed the keys to a formula one Ferrari when I was used to a twenty-miles-per-hour moped. I had no idea what I was doing with these deep, strange magicks, and it was quite possible I had condemned Wyr to eternity as a tree.

Annoying he might be, but he didn't deserve what was effectively death.

'Leave it,' said Jay, noticing the direction of my gaze. 'If it's a problem, we can work on it later.'

'Right. Fair.' We faced the tall, slender doors of the impossible tower. My heart hammered in my chest, and for a moment I could barely breathe. We'd made it. Torvaston's greatest work stood before us, and somewhere inside was the artefact that might save Farringale. And the rest of British magick into the bargain.

'Ready?' said Jay.

'No, and neither are you. But we're going anyway.'

When we advanced upon the doors, they opened themselves and swung slowly inwards upon noiseless hinges.

Magick pulsed through the floor in waves, making me shiver. I wrapped my arms around myself and strode onwards, undaunted. 'Strong stuff here,' I said to Jay. 'You're going to have some trouble.'

'I can take it,' said Jay grimly, and I reflected that he'd looked cute with horns.

If he had survived Vale, he could cope with Torvaston's tower. And if not, I'd just have to be brilliant in some unguessable way, and fix him.

No problem.

Jay and I fell silent as we went through the doors, too awed — and too wary — to speak. Beyond lay a huge hall, its walls hung with long tapestries depicting some kind of courtly scene. Troll figures, of course, and royalty, judging from the jewels and the crowns.

'Farringale,' Jay said. 'I recognise that one.'

He pointed, and I saw at once what he meant. A troll lady wearing a seventeenth-century silken gown and decked in jewels stood before a backdrop I knew at once for the great library at old Farringale.

'That one,' I said, nudging Jay. On the opposite wall, a proud-looking troll king posed in a throne room. I'd seen that crown before. 'Torvaston himself?' I suggested.

'I don't know why I don't have twenty-foot-tall portraits of myself in *my* hallway,' said Jay.

'Opportunity missed,' I agreed.

'There's still time.'

Pup did a speedy circuit of the hall, nose to the ground, tail wagging. I watched her in case she picked up any interesting scents, but she did not appear interested in anything much; she returned to me, and sat grinning. 'Pup,' I said. 'Find the thing.'

'Try being a bit less specific, if you can,' said Jay. 'You're not being quite confusing enough.'

'The *thing*,' I said. 'The magickal silver thing, the— oh, curse it. What do you suppose Torvaston called it?'

'The Work in Progress,' said Jay.

'The Saviour of Enclaves and Britains,' I said. 'Find the Saviour, Goodie.'

She sat, tongue lolling, and panted.

'We're on our own.'

Jay's smile faded as he looked around the echoing hall, and took in the number of doors leading off into parts unknown. 'Much as I would love to explore every inch of this place, it would take us about three weeks.'

'Which we don't have,' I said, watching him carefully for signs of magickal disorder. 'You'll be scrambled egg inside of twenty-four hours.'

'There is that. Also, Ancestria Magicka apparently knows about this valley, thanks to Wyr. They're bound to show up eventually.'

A point I had forgotten, in all the turmoil. Where *were* they? The last I'd heard, Fenella Beaumont — and an unspecified number of her associates — had been banished from this Britain by an irate Melmidoc, and sent to... one of the others. Had they managed to return?

If they had, where were they?

If they hadn't... how long would it be before they did?

'We need to be long gone before they show up,' I said.

'You think?'

'Right. Where in this town-sized tower might Torvaston hide his priceless life's work?'

'Judging from the look of this hall, the tower had some ceremonial function; it wasn't just a workshop,' said Jay. 'So not in any of the central areas, most like.'

'Nowhere ornate, and dripping in gold.' That would disappoint Goodie. 'Cellar, or attic?' I suggested, thinking of Home, and particularly of Orlando. There was something of a precedent for hiding the crazy stuff in one or the other of those two.

Jay pointed up. 'Griffins,' he said succinctly.

'Yes. Where better to develop, and test, a griffin-substitute than in the middle of a gigantic griffin nest?'

Jay sighed, and squared his shoulders. 'Why do so many of our missions come down to invading griffin lairs and praying we don't get eaten?'

'That's actually quite new,' I said. 'Terrible timing on your part.'

'No griffins on past missions?'

'Not too many, no. Ogres and unicorns and alikats, though. Some of them rabid.'

'Yours is an interesting job.'

'*Our* job, Jay.' I set off towards the nearest door, Pup trotting along beside me. 'Stairs. Help me.'

'Stairs, or an elevator, like outside?' said Jay. 'Why bother climbing when you can have magickal uplift?'

'What's the betting the roof can only be accessed by a secret lift at the top of a secret lift at the top of a secret lift?'

'See, that's what I like so much about you,' said Jay, checking and dismissing a few more doors. 'Your relentless optimism.'

'What can I say, years of practice... oh, here we are.' A long corridor lay beyond one of the doors, at the end of which loomed the kind of alcove that had *way up* written in some indefinable way all over it. Exquisite, of course, but it had the look of an elevator shaft about it. Straight-sided, symmetrical, blank. Stone floor.

I started down it. Pup, developing one of her random fits of enthusiasm, broke into a run and barrelled on ahead of me.

And vanished in a puff of mist, halfway down the passage.

I stopped dead in shock. 'Goodie?' I called.

Nothing moved.

'Where's she gone?' said Jay, catching up with me.

'I... don't know. She vanished.' I advanced slowly upon the innocent-seeming spot on the floor that had whisked Goodie away, and stood just shy of it. I couldn't see anything that might explain where she had gone, or how. The floor was smooth, pale starstone, like everything else.

Jay shrugged. 'Only one way to find out.'

'What way is that?' I said, hoping he had some sliver of esoteric knowledge I'd missed. After all, he was our resident expert on unusual and spectacular modes of magickal travel.

'Channel our inner Ves,' he said. 'And hope for the best.' With which words, he took a step forward, and planted his feet squarely upon the mischievous stretch of floor.

'Jay—' I said, reaching for him.

My hand closed upon empty air.

I rolled my eyes skywards. 'What,' I said under my breath, 'have I *done*?' I've created a monster.

Or an evil twin.

Ah, well.

I took a step forward of my own, braced for impact.

There wasn't one. I wafted away on a wisp of mist, lighter than air, and disappeared into the depths of Torvaston's tower.

9

Whatever swept me away in Torvaston's tower felt like a species of Waymastery, though I had never before heard of the kind that operated on an involuntary target. Or that could achieve the process so smoothly. Not to disparage Jay's skill; he does remarkable things with the pale, faded stuff we call "magick" in our Britain. But this was something else. Even the henge complexes weren't quite so seamless.

'Jay,' I began, once reality solidified around me and I'd stopped moving. 'How do you think this works? I mean, even the complexes require some kind of token, though maybe that's more to do with tax revenue than—' I stopped, because I abruptly realised I was alone. Neither Jay nor Goodie were anywhere in evidence.

I steadied myself, and took a long look around. I had been dropped in the middle of a room the size of a hay barn. Oceans of space opened up around me. I couldn't immediately decide what the chamber was for. Bookcases were in evidence, running from floor to ceiling, which suggested a library, except that there were nowhere near enough of them. One wall featured a row of high tables which reminded me of those in Orlando's workshop, but their surfaces were bare. The far end of the room sported enormous armchairs upholstered in silk, elegant little tables, and plush rugs strewn about the plain oak-boarded floor. At the other end, great crystal cabinets rose some eight or ten feet high, their doors shut, and a complicated chandelier hung from the ceiling, its lights composed of jewels in the same shades as Torvaston's compass.

Not a sound disturbed the dense silence. It was the same stillness we had experienced in old Farringale, the kind resulting from a profound absence of life.

Like Farringale, it showed no other signs of long abandonment. Shafts of sunlight shone through the long windows, illuminating clear, dust-free air. No cobwebs drifted down from the ceiling. The luxurious upholstery of those grand armchairs was untouched by time, and the carpets were pristine.

Hardly surprising, I supposed. The enchantments that lingered at old Farringale must have been the work of Torvaston's court; of course they would have brought those magicks with them.

I felt a moment's unease, though, at all these parallels. What else did Torvaston's tower have in common with old Farringale? Why was this place abandoned, and so-long sealed to the outside world? I thought of Alban and Emellana outside, and fervently hoped that the same fate as Farringale had not befallen this place. If the rocky promontory upon which this tower was built was infested with ortherex, they were in danger.

Probably it was lucky they had been obliged to stay outside.

'Stop gawking, Ves,' I murmured, and forced my feet to move. I could worry later about my companions, and time would soon tell where Jay and Goodie had ended up. Investigation beckoned, and I'd better get on with it.

Being me, I went first to the nearest bookcase. A perfunctory perusal revealed a slew of texts, mostly hand-written. None of them in any language I could read.

'Mauf,' I said, retrieving him. 'If you'd be so kind? The scholars of Mandridore don't have nearly enough to do already.'

'Madam, I would be delighted,' said Mauf, as I placed him on a low shelf.

I could swear I heard him giggle.

'Good stuff?' I said.

'Delicious,' he purred.

What might rank as *delicious* in Mauf's odd little world, I judged it best not to enquire into. 'Have fun,' I told him. 'But if you can make it quite quick, that would be great. We are, as ever, pressed for time.'

Mauf rustled his pages in a sigh. 'Great work cannot be rushed, Miss Vesper.'

'Nonetheless, you always manage it somehow. Thanks, Mauf.'

He did not reply. I hoped it was because he was absorbed in the task of soaking up knowledge, not because he was offended with me.

Then I wondered how it had come about that I worried over the tender feelings of a book. And considered this normal, to boot.

'Life doesn't get any simpler, does it?' I said to the empty air as I wandered off to look at the cabinets. They were locked, of course, every one, and I could see nothing of their contents through the frosted glass doors.

Nothing else of any interest beckoned, and I stopped, nonplussed. The place had the look of a workroom about it, excepting perhaps the plush luxury of the armchair nook. But if it was Torvaston's old inventing room, standing in it wasn't helping me much. Whatever he and his colleagues might once have worked on was long gone. Or well hidden.

I went to a window, and glanced out. I was much higher up the tower, the view told me that much. But how close I was to the tower-top rooms, I could not tell.

'Mauf,' I said. 'Time to explore. How are you getting along?'

'I will need at least an hour,' Mauf told me coolly.

'We don't have an hour. Can you prioritise?'

'Which ones would you like me to prioritise?'

'The... most interesting ones?'

'Please elaborate on how you are defining the word "interesting" in this context.'

'Um. The most important? No, don't say it. I don't know. Carry on.'

The silence that followed was broken by the sound of approaching footsteps, and I felt a surge of relief. 'Jay,' I said as the door opened. 'Where did you get to— oh!' Halfway to the door, I stopped dead, for the person coming through it was not Jay.

Nor was he human.

'Sorry,' I said numbly, paralysed with shock. Two minutes ago I had been certain that the tower was deserted; the absolute lack of signs of life, together with the deep silence, had equally proclaimed it. As had Wyr's assertion that nobody had got inside in centuries.

But here was a living person, a troll, clad in the fashions of eighty or so years ago but very much alive. Elderly, judging from his white hair and stooped posture, though his face was largely unlined. He stared back at me with a shock to mirror my own, and stammered something I could not understand.

'Apologies,' I said, moving forward again. 'I would not have barged in had I known I was intruding on somebody's home — though to be quite truthful, I did not perfectly intend to be up here at all. I'm Cordelia Vesper, a... scholar.' I held out my hand.

He did not immediately take it, nor did he speak again. I found myself scrutinised by a pair of lively, but wary, grey eyes, with a shrewdness to his glance that made me most uncomfortable.

'I must say,' he said at last. 'Treasure-hunters have changed a great deal in recent years.' He spoke lightly accented English, with a hesitation that suggested he did not often use the language.

'I'm not a treasure hunter,' I said firmly, choosing not to mention that I had brought one such to his doorstep. Even if I had also turned him into a charmingly unthreatening tree.

I was awarded a handshake at last, though a tentative one. 'And yet,' he said, 'you have contrived to find your way straight into the workshops.'

'Not entirely by choice. I was on the ground floor, and then somehow whisked up here—'

'Oh?' he interrupted, and looked at me afresh. Was it my imagination, or had the suspicion increased? 'And how came that about?'

'I do not know, sir. I wish I did.' I hesitated, on the point of telling him about Jay and Pup. Should I?

Yes. Something told me that to err on the side of honesty might be wise.

'I came here with an associate,' I said. 'And a... dog.' Curse it, if he found out that the dog in question was a treasure-sniffing nose-for-gold, he would never believe that I wasn't a thief. 'I do not know whereabouts they have ended up.'

'Outside, most likely,' he said, with a trace of amusement. 'That is where intruders are usually sent.'

Oh. Then I was on my own in here.

'The question remains,' he said, looking keenly at me. 'How is it that you were not? And indeed, how came you to pass the wards at all?'

If by "wards" he meant the spectacular illusions which disguised the tower as an impregnable mountain, I was dying to ask him *all* about that.

But courtesies first.

'Regarding the second question,' I said, 'I have this.' I showed him the compass. 'I have three other associates outside. We took down the wards between us. Though we did not expect to encounter... occupants.'

Why hadn't they? Because the enclave had been founded hundreds of years ago. Because according to Wyr, the door hadn't opened in living memory; no one had got in, and presumably no one had been known to come out either. Because I was used to the echoing decay of lost civilisations, in particular Farringale, and to imagine that someone might still be living in *this* one had seemed unthinkable.

My unexpected interlocutor had gone very quiet. He held out his hand for Torvaston's compass, and with only a slight hesitation, I gave it over to him. It lay in his palm, untouched, and he gazed at it as though he beheld a miracle.

Slowly, carefully, he stroked a thumb over its surface.

'Well, now,' he said softly. 'And I never thought to see its like again.'

It struck me that my possession of the compass might prove to be the answer to both of his questions. If the henge complexes operated based on something in the traveller's possession, might not the tower's Waymastered enchantments also respond to something I held? If I hadn't had the compass with me, I might well have ended up booted outside.

Which led my thoughts back to the topic of Jay. He'd had the snuff box with him. So, then. Was he outside, or somewhere else in the tower?

My new troll friend (hopefully) looked up. 'I think you had better tell me how you came by this,' he said, and a hint of steel had crept into his tone. 'Was this stolen?'

Tricky question. 'It— well— no, although also yes. It's complicated—'

His eyes narrowed, and I stopped gabbling and held up my hands.

'I work for the Troll Court at Mandridore, on the sixth Britain,' I said hastily. 'We're here at their instigation. We took that— *object*— from old Farringale-that-was, with Their Majesties' permission, so in that sense it isn't stolen. And somewhere in the valley out there is Prince Alban, next heir to the troll throne.'

All of this came out in a rush, and was met with silence.

Then: 'And what is your aim, in infiltrating this tower?'

I swallowed. 'We— perhaps ought to have a longer conversation about all this.'

I expected more of the inquisition, perhaps greater hostility. To my surprise, instead, he gave a mournful sigh, his fingers closing slightly around the compass. 'We knew it would come,' he said, so quietly I wondered whether he was talking to me at all. 'Well, and it has come.'

'May I... ask what you mean?' I said.

'His Majesty's kin,' he said. 'We hoped you would not find us. And at such a distance of years, it seemed unlikely that any of you now would.'

'But... why?'

'Because you would doubtless come looking for his work, and... it was not his wish that you should ever find it.'

10

So MUCH FOR MY brilliant theory. Torvaston came here to perfect his magick-regulating device, I'd thought, so that he could someday go home and repair the damage he had helped to cause at Farringale. True, I had come up with no ideas as to why he never *had* gone back — except that the device, perhaps, never worked.

To hear that he had actively chosen *not* to go back, and indeed to hide the thing from everyone who might come looking for him... well, that changed things.

'I don't understand,' I said.

The elderly troll straightened. 'If I tell you that your purpose in coming here cannot be fulfilled, and Torvaston's work will never be released to you. Do you, then, still wish to ask questions of me?'

'Of course,' I said, frowning.

He nodded once, and held out his hand, Torvaston's compass still tucked into his palm. As I took it, he tightened his fingers briefly around mine, before releasing me. I hoped it was a gesture of goodwill. His scrutiny of me appeared, now, more curious than suspicious. 'The sixth Britain,' he mused. 'But Torvaston always said that magick would decline there, and you— do not appear to bear out that theory.'

Not bristling with magick as I was, no. I stood there as his (temporary) equal, a natural part of all that lovely magickal flow. 'It's complicated,' I said.

His lips curved in a faint smile. 'I am the seventeenth Earl Evemer,' he said. 'But you may call me Luan.'

I made him my best Milady-curtsey, which prompted another smile. Then I ruined it by saying, 'Call me Ves.'

QUARTER OF AN HOUR later, I sat in a quiet parlour some floors below with Earl Evemer, being plied with good things. Always my favourite part of any mission.

'You are not, then, here alone?' I enquired, somewhere in the midst of my third scone.

'Oh, no. We are not so numerous as once we were, of course, but twenty-one wardens remain, along with our families.'

'Wardens?'

'Our lineages were tasked with the care and protection of the tower and its contents, before His Majesty died. Some few of us have died out in the intervening centuries, but enough remain.'

Seventy or eighty people, perhaps, in a building the size of a small town. No wonder it felt deserted, or some parts of it did. Here on the lower floors, I'd seen signs enough of habitation, though we had not yet encountered anyone else.

'You never bring in anyone from outside?'

'Outside?' he echoed, aghast. 'Never.'

I thought about everything I had seen beyond this serene enclave forgotten by time, and couldn't wonder at it. Twenty-one wardens and their families could never be enough to protect the tower from the likes of Wyr, and his trade-partners of Vale. Hungry for profit, morally moribund, and devoid of respect for either history or consequence, they'd decimate the place.

But, how isolated an existence. And the ultimate fate of everyone who lived here must be a final and irrevocable decline.

I was growing tired of that general theme.

Earl Evemer — Luan — munched his way slowly through a sweet roll, his gaze fixed somewhere on the middle distance. I didn't rush him. Having just given him the speedy low-down on everything that had led me to his tower, my next duty was to leave him a moment to think it over.

And devour a couple more delicacies in the process. Gods, but I was *hungry*.

By the time he again spoke, I was happily replete and dozing off in my dangerously comfortable armchair. A fire burned in the grate, around which we and our tea-table were arranged. Watching the flames, I'd been close to gliding off to sleep.

'One or two points do not perfectly make sense,' said Luan at length, startling me awake.

I sat up quickly, trying to look alert. 'Mm,' I said intelligently. 'Um. Yes.' I tapped the compass on the arm of my chair.

'Yes,' said Luan. 'That is the salient point.'

'You don't know how this came to be at Farringale?'

'I did not know that any had been left there.'

'Plus the key to the door, tucked inside a scroll-case. And on the inside of that case was a map of the mountains within which this enclave is hidden. Either Torvaston himself returned once to Farringale and left these things there, or he sent someone else to do it. So, if he did not want his work to be unearthed by his descendants, why did he leave us the means to follow him?'

Luan stared at the compass. 'I cannot answer that. But, Ves, you should know...'

I waited, but he did not finish the sentence. 'What should I know?' I prompted.

He looked at me, and I read unease and something like guilt in his eyes. 'His Majesty's... project,' he said.

'The, er, regulator?'

'If you would like to call it that, yes. It... well, it no longer exists.'

I almost dropped my tea cup. 'Tell me I heard that wrong.'

Luan shook his head. 'The records state that His Majesty came to regret the project,' he said, and fell silent again.

Much as I could sympathise with his predicament, I did not really have a lot of time to waste while he wrestled with himself. 'Because it never worked?' I prompted.

He blinked. 'Oh, no. It wasn't that it did not work.'

I reminded myself to breathe. 'You mean... do you mean that it *did* work, or the fact that it didn't was not the source of Torvaston's regret?'

'It worked,' he said. 'This enclave was built partly with the assistance of— it is referred to as the Heart of Hyndorin. Because, we must conclude, that is precisely what it was. Coming as you do from a diminished Britain, you might not suppose that this place is a pale shadow of its former glory. Yet, it is much faded, because the Heart is gone.'

I stared. 'The thing *worked!* Giddy gods, this changes everything.'

'Yes,' said Luan heavily. 'It did, change everything. It was too much of a success, you see. It was His Majesty's greatest pride, and as you have surmised, he *did* hope to return to Farringale with it, and reverse that enclave's destruction.

'But, others among his courtiers had different ideas. Where there is powerful magick, there will always be— avarice, and ambition. In this instance, there was not only powerful magick but the means to generate more and more of it. You may imagine, I suppose, what that repre-sented to some of the members of His Majesty's Court.'

I could not suppress a sigh. What a tired old story. 'And this is why we can't have nice things,' I said.

Luan blinked at me, and I reminded himself that he came from a society worlds away from mine. 'The Court divided into two factions,' he said. 'Torvaston's closest allies, and those who came to oppose his ideas. The Heart became a dangerous bone of contention between them, and— matters soon grew out of hand. Much damage was done. His Majesty came to doubt his *own* plans, in the wake of this disaster, and wondered whether the very de-scendants upon whom he had expected to bestow his work might not prove unworthy of it. Placed into the wrong hands, it would do far more harm to your Britain than good. And he had been in such a position before.'

Of course, he had. He was the king whose efforts to save his kingdom had ultimately hastened its demise. He would be the last person to sail blindly into another such mistake. My heart ached at the tragedy of it, and the waste. I'd fairly castigated Wyr and his ilk for insufficient interest in the consequences of their actions; had the opposite attitude led Torvaston to destroy his irreplaceable work?

'The Heart was destroyed in 1741,' said Luan. 'At the very end of Torvaston's life. It broke his heart to do it, so they say, for he did not long survive its destruction. Those whose actions had led to his decision were expelled forever from Hyndorin. Those who remained were appointed tower wardens, to guard what was left for as long as we could.'

'Against the return of Torvaston's enemies?' I guessed.

'Yes. And everyone else.'

'Has no one else ever got in? Ever?'

Luan shifted in his chair. 'Once in a great while. We are not quite self-sufficient here; occasionally it is necessary for some of us to leave, to procure necessities, or to conduct research. Carelessness or ill luck are inevitable in time, of course, and it has sometimes happened that someone has followed one of us back inside.'

'And... what came of that?'

'We dealt with it,' he said, in a harder voice. 'And took greater care in future. It hasn't happened in a long time.'

I wanted to ask how they had *dealt with it*, exactly. No reports of successful infiltration of this Enclave had made it beyond the walls, apparently. But Luan was looking, grimly and with some sadness, at an unusual standard lamp in one corner. I'd noticed it before, for it was oddly twisted in shape, and its green silk shade tilted, almost like a bowed head.

I thought of what I had done to Wyr, and decided I did not need to know the details.

'So you see,' said Luan, returning his attention to me. 'I cannot help you fulfil your mission, for it is beyond my power.'

'Even if it was ultimately Torvaston's wish?' I said. 'Maybe he thought differently, before he died. Maybe he had a little faith in us after all.'

'Even if he did, the Heart is gone forever. There is nothing for you to take back to his successors.'

I saw that he did not much regret having to give me such a negative for an answer. Despite the evidence of the scroll-case and the compass and the key, as far as he was concerned, his ancestral king had decided the Heart was not to be entrusted to anyone ever again. He and his ancestors had dedicated their lives to protecting what was left of Torvaston's legacy. They were used to doing as he was thought to have wanted.

Also, in fairness, even the compass and scroll-case did not absolutely mean that Torvaston had changed his mind. It could have been someone else who'd taken them to Farringale, after his death. It wasn't a likely explanation, but nor was it impossible.

'I understand,' I said graciously, even as my mind was busy working on a way around the problem.

An idea occurred to me, and I sat up. 'Luan,' I said. 'One question.'

'Yes?'

'I suppose there isn't any chance that Torvaston lied?'

'Lied?' he repeated, with strong disapproval.

'About destroying the Heart. You don't suppose he might have made everyone believe that he'd wrecked it, while he'd actually hidden it instead?'

'No,' said Luan, crushing my hopes. 'Its destruction was witnessed by his most loyal courtiers. The materials that went into making it were redistributed, and crafted into other artefacts, many of which are still here. There can be no doubt that the Heart is gone.'

I sagged back in my chair again, disappointed.

But. The Heart itself might be gone, but someone had built the thing in the first place, and someone had possibly kept records of the process. And guess who had a friend in the library/workshop upstairs, cheerfully soaking up every word the trolls of Hyndorin had written?

'I do believe we are about to have company,' said Luan, his eyes going faraway. 'Someone of your acquaintance, I hope.'

In other words, someone unfamiliar to him. I had only an instant to think of Jay before the door swung open, and someone charged into the room, stopping just short of colliding with Luan's chair.

The newcomer was about Jay's height and had his colouring, but otherwise the resemblances were few. This man was sprouting feathers, and a pair of incorporeal wings hovered behind him. His long fingers curled under like claws, and they were tipped with talons.

I did not want to look too closely at his face, because I was fairly sure he had more beak than mouth and good *heavens*.

He was wearing a familiar jacket.

'Jay,' I said. 'I don't wish to alarm you, but you appear to be turning into a griffin.'

11

'Hippogriff, I think,' said Luan calmly, and pointed to Jay's feet.

Hooves. Dead giveaway.

Jay said something beaky.

'Oh, dear,' I sighed.

'Your associate?' said Luan.

'Yes. And I would love to know where he's been this past hour or so, but I think I'll have to get him out of here to find out. He was okay outside.'

'Magickal dissonance,' said Luan, nodding. 'It has been harder to maintain a balance since the Heart was lost.' His eyes narrowed, fixed upon me. 'How is it that your companion is so much affected, while you are not?'

I had not yet got around to telling him that part of my increasingly complicated story. 'It all started in Vale,' I said, trying unsuccessfully to soothe a visibly alarmed Jay.

'Vale?' echoed Luan sharply. 'What were you doing up there?'

'Looking for this place. Torvaston's map depicted both the valley of the Vales of Wonder, and the Hyndorin Mountains, and we went to the other one first. It's... interesting up there.'

Luan gave a faint snort, but did not offer any further comment.

'Well, and we were all losing our collective... er, marbles in Vale. It's *way* too intensely magickal for a feeble crowd from a magickal backwater. We were given these disgusting unicorn potions to drink, and that helped. For a while.'

'And then what?' said Luan, when I fell silent.

How to explain the rest?

All in a giant rush, and hope for unusual mental acuity in my auditor. Go.

'We went to the top of Mount Vale and there's *major* griffin and unicorn activity up there by the way, not without a certain amount of forced labour, and we were kind of in trouble and we wanted to release all the shiny beasts. So I took out my mother's magickal lyre of fabulousness and it sort of adopted me and I came out of that experience soaked in magick up to my eyeballs.'

Luan looked at me in silence.

'That part has yet to go away,' I finished. 'Hence, I am okay in here but Jay is not. Which is rather the reverse of the way things were back in Scarborough, when everyone else was okay and I existed on the point of imminent explosion.'

Luan nodded slowly. 'It is many years since any of us were in Vale,' he mused. 'You have guessed, I suppose, the connection?'

'No,' I said. 'I don't—' I paused, and thought. Jay had taken a seat beside me, and I realised I was absently stroking his arm. He had soft feathers. I have no idea if it was more soothing to him or to me.

Connections between the enclaves of Hyndorin and Vale. Torvaston had clearly had an interest in the latter, even if he had not chosen it for his headquarters. His scroll-case told us that much. But if he hadn't settled there, and his successors at Hyndorin never went there anymore, what possible link could there be?

Jay said something, his beak clattering, and gesticulated.

'How long has there been a settlement in Vale?' I said. 'In Torvaston's day, it appears to have been known as the Vales of Wonder, which is suggestive of an area of natural magickal intensity. We were surprised to find a town, when we went there.'

Jay said something else, and I even caught a word or two. 'Yes,' I agreed. 'Some parts of the town did appear to be very old.'

Luan smiled faintly. 'Very good. Yes, the settlement there is not so old as this one, but nearly so. It dates from the mid eighteenth century.'

Or, around the same time that the Heart of Hyndorin was destroyed. 'That is where Torvaston's disgraced courtiers went,' I guessed. 'The ones who opposed him, and were kicked out.'

Luan inclined his head. 'It has been built according to very different values. I am disappointed to hear that little has improved since those days.'

Jay rolled his eyes, and slumped back into the cushions in an attitude of despair.

I patted his hand. 'Hippogriffs are noble creatures.'

Whatever Jay said next sounded suspiciously like a curse.

'I may be able to help,' said Luan. 'But first, I would like to hear more about that lyre.'

'It's an Yllanfalen artefact. Its primary purpose is to select a king or queen for Ygranyllon, the kingdom of its origin, and it's been doing that for centuries. Supposedly it was created by one of their early kings, who the Yllanfalen revere almost as some kind of god, and it's made out of skysilver or moonsilver or some such fancifully-named thing.' I paused for effect, and added: 'Or, what

His Majesty Torvaston seems to have referred to, slightly less imaginatively, as "magickal silver".'

That got his lordship's attention. 'Magickal silver?' he repeated, and sat up in his chair. 'That is— remarkable.'

'Just like the Heart, am I right?'

His expression became guarded. 'I cannot say.'

'I get it. You can neither confirm nor deny.' I held up the compass. 'And am I much mistaken in thinking this thing has a few moonsilver parts to it, too?'

Luan's lips twitched. 'I cannot say.'

'Mm.'

Jay held out the snuff-box, in the palm of one clawed hand. 'That, too?' I said, looking at him.

He nodded furiously. I gathered that his possession of the box had taken him somewhere quite interesting indeed. We really needed to get that beak off his face.

'The key, too,' I said. 'So it appears that this substance, by whatever name it is known, is capable of serious business when it comes to magick.'

'Because of which, it is almost impossible to find any longer,' said Luan. 'There was a seam of it in the environs of Vale, long ago, which is perhaps a partial explanation of Torvaston's interest in it. Most likely that particular source was exhausted before the town was settled.'

'Are there any more known?'

'Not at this time. Nor is it possible, any longer, to acquire unworked examples of the metal. Therefore,' and he looked seriously at me, 'I need hardly tell you how incredibly valuable is that lyre. Its properties do not surprise me, if it is made entirely from magickal silver. There are people who would kill you in a heartbeat for possession of so much of it.'

I thanked my lucky stars for my odd obsession with the lyre. If it were not for that, Jay would not have had reason to hide it, and we might have been waltzing all over the fifth Britain carrying more magickal goodness than our collective lives were worth.

'Question,' I said. 'Have you heard before of the silver's having a... mesmerising effect, on some people?

'Is this what you meant when you referred to its having "adopted" you?' asked Luan.

'Sort of. That didn't happen until I picked it up and played it. Before that, I had trouble resisting the temptation to do so. I practically had to be restrained.'

'Hmm.' Luan looked me over thoughtfully. 'Would it interest you to know that His Majesty was said to have a similar fascination with the stuff?'

'Why yes, it *would*.'

'History does not say why, however. I am unsure whether the reason for it was ever known.'

'Curse it.'

'Does it bother you so very much?'

'It didn't, until I played the thing. Now I am too explosively magickal to go home, and *that* bothers me quite a lot.' I did not add that I felt condemned to Torvaston's own fate. Exiled from my own Britain, and obliged to stay forever in a place like Hyndorin or Vale. I mean, it was a perfectly lovely tower, but nothing to compare to the familiar comforts and chaos of Home.

A swift stab of intense homesickness took me aback, and I paused to swallow it down.

'Magickal silver is sought after for more than one reason,' said Luan. 'Partly for its propensity to absorb magickal energy. It is only a personal theory, but I believe that may have been the original source for His Majesty's ideas.'

'Yes!' I said. 'That makes sense. Perhaps he thought it could be used to absorb the excess at old Farringale, and... undrown it.'

'Perhaps so,' Luan allowed. 'But it also, as you have discovered, has the capacity to expend energy in interesting ways — specifically, without much depleting stored magicks. In other words, it absorbs and also generates, in a cycle reminiscent of the behaviour of nesting griffins.'

I nodded. This coincided, more or less, with our own ideas. 'And Torvaston himself?' I guessed.

Luan eyed me. 'I may be wrong, but your condition could prove confirmation of an idea I have long toyed with.'

'Torvaston was a kind of human griffin,' I said. 'His personal papers suggest as much.'

'Yes. And he may have become so in the same way that you have. Through close contact with, and manipulation of, a charged source of magickal silver.'

That agreed with everything Alban had told us. 'Was he... ever known to have, um, stopped being a human griffin?'

'No.'

Damnit. I really was stuck forever.

'The lyre, perhaps, may prove both curse and cure,' suggested Luan. 'But in the meantime, let us tend to your unfortunate colleague.' He stood up — but then his eyes flicked to me, and he said, 'Or perhaps *you* may do so.'

'Me?' I echoed dumbly.

'Imbalance is the problem. Your friend — you called him Jay? — is out of his magickal depth, here, and is therefore vulnerable to interference.'

'Magickal shot straight to the heart?' I suggested.

Luan blinked, nonplussed. 'If you were to share some of what you call your *excess* magick with your colleague, it may stabilise him.'

I liked this idea much better than chugging unicorn organs. 'But will it make him like me?' I asked, struck with sudden alarm. Jay might have talked of staying in the fifth Britain forever, but absolutely had not been serious. I didn't want to condemn him to share my exile.

'Were the effects of those "potions" you spoke of permanent?' said Luan, with an amused smile.

'Strictly temporary.'

'Then I believe you may proceed with confidence.'

All well and good, but how exactly did one go about magickally supercharging one's friends? 'No offence, Jay, but I'm not giving up a kidney for this.'

He gave me a flat, hard look. It probably said, *if you imagine I'm drinking any potion made from your internal organs, you're a madwoman.*

Good that we were on the same page.

I thought back a few hours, to our madcap journey up to Hyndorin. Jay had hauled me through the Ways via physical contact, in spite of the fact that touching me produced clear signs of magickal disorder.

But that was outside, where Jay was comfortable and I was not. I'd messed him up because proximity to me had thrown his magickal balance out of whack.

Maybe I was overthinking this. Maybe, in here, all I needed to do was touch him, and I'd throw his magickal balance *into* whack. Or something.

'Righto, Jay,' I said. 'There's nothing else for it. It's hug time.' I held out my arms, smiling beatifically.

I received a look of narrow-eyed suspicion in return.

'Look,' I said. 'Do you want to spend eternity as a hippogriff or not?'

Damn him, he actually thought it over.

Then he swept me up in a bone-creaking hug, the kind which lifted me a couple of inches off the floor.

'Whoa,' I said. 'Having a beak isn't *that* bad.'

Apparently it was, for he did not release me until I'd passed out from lack of oxygen.

Okay, no. He didn't release me until the feathers were on the retreat and the beak was gone and those weird incorporeal wings had faded into the aether.

Then he dropped me. '*Finally*,' he said, and I smiled into his reassuringly normal Jay-face once more.

He did not smile back. 'Ves, do you have any idea what that hound of yours has gone and done?'

I stopped smiling. 'Pup? No, why? Is she okay?'

'Oh, she's fine.' He began, oddly, to laugh. Mild hysteria. 'She's done what she usually does, and scuttled her wriggly little way to a stash of treasure.'

'That doesn't sound *too* bad,' I said cautiously.

'I'll give you a hint. It's silver, and there's quite a bit of it.'

'What— wait, how did she not get ported outside? I thought you said—' I looked at Luan, and was struck by the gobsmacked look on his face. 'Not relevant. Lord Evemer? Are you all right?'

He visibly swallowed, and said in a constrained voice: 'Did you say silver?'

12

'Not just any silver,' said Jay helpfully. 'I'm no expert, but I'm pretty sure it's the same kind as the lyre.'

'That is entirely—' said Luan, and stopped. 'What kind of a hound circumvents my defences and finds its way straight to the most valuable artefacts in the building?'

'She's a nose-for-gold,' I said quickly, remembering too late that I had glossed over Pup's presence before.

His face set into disapproving lines. 'I think you said you were *not* treasure hunters?'

'We aren't. It's just Pup that has a few bad habits...'

'And what manner of scholar keeps a nose-for-gold?'

A fair question. 'She's an academic oddity where we come from,' I said, trying my best smile.

'We aren't here to steal your silver,' said Jay irritably. 'We came looking for Torvaston's project, that's all.'

'That,' said Luan in a terrible voice, '*is* our silver.'

Jay blinked. '...Oh.'

So the "Heart" was a dismantled pile of Silver with a capital S, and it was lying in a storeroom somewhere in this largely-empty tower. I remembered myself telling Wyr he was welcome to plunder at will once we got inside, and winced. All right, I hadn't thought the place would prove to be inhabited, but that was the best excuse I had for my reckless promise. A cache of something so frighteningly valuable and powerful must never be permitted to fall into the hands of someone like him.

Earl Evemer and his compatriots had successfully protected it for centuries. It was *our* unauthorised presence here that put it at risk.

Way to go, team.

'We should go,' I said.

Jay looked sharply at me. 'Go?'

'What we came for no longer exists,' I said. 'Mission over. We can go back to Mandridore and tell them it's a no go.'

'We?'

For a second, I'd forgotten my no-fly state. 'Erm.' I looked around. 'Where is Pup? You left her with the Silver?'

'If you'd like to try prising her off that stuff, be my guest.'

I sighed. 'I am very sorry,' I said to Luan. 'If we can retrieve my disgraceful thief of a Pup—' (and, come to think of it, my intellectual thief of a book) '—We will get off your lawn, and stop complicating your day.'

Luan held up a hand. 'Not so fast.'

I stared. 'What?'

'I would like a look at that lyre, please.'

I dithered. I could hardly blame him for asking, but... I did not want to hand it over.

Then again, we stood here swearing blind we weren't there to rob the place, and expected him to just trust our word, despite all apparent evidence to the contrary. It would be unbecoming to refuse to trust him for even five minutes with *our* articles of value.

I looked at Jay. He had hidden the thing; it was for him to decide whether or not to reveal it.

He looked quizzically back at me. *I'm the new guy,* his face (probably) said. *Why are you making me decide, o mentor?*

Because your guess is as good as mine, I signalled back.

He shrugged, and set the snuff box down. Which reminded me. 'Hey, where in the tower did you get swept off to?'

'Some kind of bedchamber,' he said, counting downwards through the buttons on his shirt. 'Or a museum. The place was practically preserved in aspic.'

A choked sound emerged from Luan.

'You okay?' I said.

'A grand chamber?' asked Luan.

'Fit for a king,' said Jay. 'Probably literally.'

Luan groped for his chair, and sat back down. 'His Majesty's private quarters.'

I studied him. He'd turned white. 'Why's that so shocking?'

'Because,' he said faintly, 'those rooms have been inaccessible since Torvaston died.' He lunged suddenly, *way* fast for such an old man, and scooped up the snuff box that Jay had set down on the arm of my chair. 'This must have belonged to His Majesty,' he said, and his voice shook. Then he chuckled, though the almost maniacal glint in his eye took all the mirth out of the sound. 'Not that we have nothing left of his personal possessions, but none of them have ever worked. Because he attuned the charm to... to a *snuff box.*'

'And what a snuff box!' said Jay, producing the damned lyre with a flourish.

All thoughts leaked out of my foolish brain, and time stopped. I stared like an idiot at the pretty thing, its curving frame gleaming like moon-touched silver, its strings rippling like sun-touched waters, and the cursed thing *sang* to me. The melody reverberated through my bones, and I knew I would remember those notes for the rest of my life.

Magick pulsed around me. I no longer saw Earl Evemer's handsome, old-fashioned parlour, or not in such prosaic terms as walls and furniture and fireplaces. I saw the world as a flow of magick, colourless yet shimmering with all the colours in the world. Jay was a firework throwing off sparks — my doing, perhaps. Luan blended in, seamlessly, like a single thread in a complex, perfect tapestry.

I do not know how I might have appeared, for I could not see myself. But I felt right. Slotted in like the final piece in a jigsaw puzzle. Powerful.

I do not know what happened between the moment of Jay's waving the lyre around, and the moment when he hid it behind its glamour once more. I came awake with a start, to find Jay looking unperturbed (good, Earl Evemer had not tried to make off with the lyre), and his lordship seated once again in his deep armchair, looking six ways shaken.

'I would like very much to see His Majesty's chambers,' said Luan.

'You do have the snuff box,' I pointed out. He still held it clutched in his left hand.

His fingers opened as I spoke, and he offered it back to us. 'And I have taken it without your permission.'

'Do you need our permission?' I said, uncertain. 'It more rightly belongs to you than to us.'

But Luan shook his head. 'I may not know why, but Torvaston had his reasons for leaving these things in your

Britain. And he was *of* your world, not ours. If you are here at the behest of his natural heirs, then I will not lay claim to this box.'

I exchanged a look with Jay. 'I can't think of a single reason to object to your using it,' I said.

'Neither can I,' agreed Jay.

Not that I didn't suffer a moment's disquiet. Why *had* Torvaston locked everyone out of his rooms, and left the key in our Britain instead?

But I couldn't afford to start doubting Luan's motives now. Apart from anything, I badly wanted to see those rooms, too.

'Let's go,' I said. 'Oh,' I added casually, 'And I'd like to stop by that workshop on the way there. I may have, um, left something behind.'

TEN MINUTES LATER, I stood with Luan and Jay at a crossroads in the network of passages that ran throughout the tower. These four-way junctions functioned as transport points, Luan informed us, provided you either knew how to manipulate them, or you were carrying something that served as a token.

That didn't explain how one of them had swept Pup away, but since no one was likely to have any explanation to offer for Goodie's peculiar brand of larking about, I chose not to raise the issue.

Mauf lay snug in my shoulder bag. Snug and *smug*. 'Miss Vesper!' he had greeted me as I stole into the workshop. 'I lay my intellectual riches at your exquisite feet.'

I'd stopped, surprised into immobility. 'I beg your pardon?'

'I,' he said proudly, 'have been *very* busy.'

If I didn't know it to be impossible, I would have said he sounded drunk. Drunk on knowledge? Intoxicated by academia? Mauf had drunk deeply from the Well of Wisdom, and was now high as a kite.

I gave his front cover a soothing pat as I picked him up. 'Just out of interest, could you actually read any of those texts?'

'Not a word.' He giggled.

I gave up.

He now lay asleep (supposedly) in the bottom of the bag. Once in a while I heard something like a stray chortle from somewhere in the vicinity of my right elbow.

Best to ignore it.

'Forgive me,' said Luan, paused on the brink of taking the plunge into Torvaston's Royal Apartments. 'Is your bag... laughing?'

'Long story,' I said.

He just looked at me, and I felt a bit guilty. I had just used Mauf to thieve Hyndorin secrets, even if I hadn't taken anything of material value. I had no business standing there like butter wouldn't melt.

Then again, if the snuff box was more rightly our property than his, because *our Britain* and *natural successors* and *representatives of the Troll Court,* yada yada, then surely works related to Torvaston's projects qualified under the same rule. Right?

Sometimes I envied Jay his utter moral certainty. It did make him a bit of a stick in the mud sometimes, but at least he was spared these exhausting bouts of wrestling with his conscience.

It being rather too late in the day to set about being a goody two-shoes, I abandoned that line of thought.

Luan was hesitating.

'Everything all right?' I said, when time passed and he did not move.

'Yes,' he said. 'It is only that... no one here has seen these rooms in hundreds of years. Their very existence has become the province of more myth than fact.'

'That makes it exciting,' I offered, bouncing a bit on my toes.

He nodded, and straightened purposefully. I wasn't fooled. His hands were shaking.

People really revered Torvaston, didn't they? I hoped he was the kind of person who deserved all this adulation. As far as I could determine, his track record was a bit too varied to merit it.

'He must have had a really magnetic personality,' I muttered.

'Torvaston?' said Luan. 'He was like a god.'

With which bombshell, he stepped into the crossroads vortex and vanished, sweeping Jay and I away with him.

13

To call our next destination a Royal Bedchamber would be to grossly understate the impact of the place.

It wasn't fit for a king so much as a... well, a god. In size alone, it staggered me. Okay, Torvaston was a troll, and they aren't short, but even so: how much space does one person *need*? We emerged in a chamber the approximate size of a football field (yes, I exaggerate, but not by much). Dominating the centre of that space was a bed large enough to sleep about thirty human-sized people. Its four posts were trees, crystalline and sparkling but clearly tree-shaped, and apparently alive. Canopies of cobwebby gauze hung about it, and its pillows and blankets had the kind of plushness a Ves could cheerfully sink into forever.

I've never seen an article of furniture so clearly scream *magick!*

The rest of the décor was of a piece with it. Lamps of contorted crystal hung from the ceiling and erupted from the walls, glowing under their own power; carpets covered the hardwood floor, their patterns and colours shifting as I looked at them; cabinets held artefacts safely behind glass, though every time I glanced their way I beheld a different array of objects.

Etc. If this was the lifestyle of a king in a magick-soaked enclave, I could definitely see its upside.

Luan walked through that room as though he walked in the presence of a god. His soft-footed, wide-eyed, reverential behaviour unnerved me. Did he think Torvaston was going to show up?

Was Torvaston going to show up?

'You look petrified,' Jay said, glancing at me.

I composed my features. 'It's the word "god" that did it,' I said.

'And?'

'Any sane person is terrified of gods.'

'Does that include the giddy kind you keep referring to?'

'A degree of healthy irreverence is good for a person,' I retorted.

Jay made no answer, save for his by-now-familiar eyebrow quirk that said *whatever you say, Ves.*

I shut my mouth.

Jay was right about the bedchamber more nearly resembling a museum. Like the rest of the tower (or as much as we had seen of it), it was meticulously well-kept, without a speck of dust or dirt anywhere. Considering these rooms had been sealed for centuries, however, that fact registered as highly unusual. Moreover, it had the air of a museum about it, of a place not merely dusted and swept but preserved. As though the effects of time had been, if not outright stopped, then at least slowed down.

Strong magicks indeed.

I wondered again why Torvaston had closed off this room, while apparently going to some trouble to preserve it. For whom? The chances that anyone would manage to follow his obscure trail of clues and oblique references and stray magickal bits-and-bobs were vanishingly small, which was why hundreds of years had passed before anyone had done so.

And I still felt like we were here more by some kind of fluke than by our own efforts.

Or by Milady's possible flickers of clairvoyance. After all, it was she who had manoeuvred things so that we could keep our mischievous nose-for-gold Pup. It was Pup who had retrieved the scroll-case from Farringale, and brought it to me. It was Milady again who had brought in the Baron, and through him we had forged links with the Court at Mandridore — who had sent us out here. With

Alban in pursuit, bearing just the things we needed to get into this room.

I shied away from concluding that anything like *fate* had brought us here; that would be absurd. But a somewhat manipulated run of "luck" certainly had. So then, why?

'What's in here that's important?' I said to Jay. Luan was on the other side of the room, still in a state of reverence. I half expected him to fall to his knees before an enormous, bejewelled chair that strongly resembled a throne. He'd probably die before he so much as considered sitting on it.

I, however, strongly wanted to plant my derriere on those sumptuous green velvet cushions.

I turned my face away from it, lest the temptation should overcome me.

'Important?' Jay said, frowning. 'All of it, surely.'

'As far as intriguing uses of magick go, and evidence of a delightful excess: yes. But I mean, what's important to *us* in here.'

'You mean, what would Milady want us to shamelessly make off with?'

'No!' I gasped, appalled. 'What would Milady want us to... heroically liberate in the name of magick.'

'My mistake.'

'Hint: It's unlikely to be anything with material value.'

'So not the gigantic pile of magickal silver lying in a storeroom a ways nearby.'

'Is it really gigantic?'

'Relatively speaking. It's enough to make a few lyres and snuff boxes, anyway.'

'None of it looks like it might be a conveniently flat-packed magickal regulator, I suppose?'

'Because they absolutely had IKEA for uniquely powerful artefacts in the seventeen hundreds.'

'You never know.'

He grinned. 'Yes, I do. And no, it doesn't.'

'Curse it.'

He looked around at Torvaston's glamorous bedchamber, and shrugged. 'I don't know, Ves. Everything in here is dripping in gold. It could be anything or nothing.'

Most likely nothing, I thought, though my eye lingered on those cabinets. The curiously changeable nature of the contents intrigued me a little. What better way to protect objects of unusual value, than to make it impossible to identify what each object was?

Then again, it could also be an elaborate feint. If I were prone to thieving artefacts of great power — just for instance — the so-obviously magickal nature of all those carefully stored articles would attract me greatly. I'd be inclined to empty those cabinets forthwith, and might miss something more subtle.

Like... like a secret door, for example. Secret, but not because it was hidden. More because it was so subtle. Blandly mundane in the midst of such splendour, and half-hidden behind a cabinet to boot.

'Did you go through that door?' I asked Jay, pointing.

'What door— oh.' He blinked in its general direction. 'I didn't notice it before.'

'Because you looked right past it, or conceivably because it wasn't there before?'

Jay thought. 'I honestly don't know.'

'I vote we investigate.'

'Seconded.'

But as we ventured towards the door, it melted away.

There and then gone.

Jay took this in stride, which said a lot about his experiences with the Society since he'd joined us. Disappearing doors? All in a day's work. He went up to the wall where the door had been, and felt around with his hands. 'It's really gone,' he reported.

'Right.' I did a three hundred and sixty degree turn, scanning the room.

And spotted the slithery thing skulking behind an elegant console table, not far from the throne. Chair. Whatever. 'There!' I said, and ran for it.

This time, I almost made it before it began to fade. 'No, you *don't*,' I said, and made a grab for the heavy silver (or Silver?) doorknob.

My fingers closed around it, and I yelped. It was *cold*, like ice fresh from the freezer. It hurt to touch it, but I grimly hung on, and threw my full body weight behind my efforts to haul it open.

Without much effect. A five-foot-barely-anything Ves doesn't weigh all that much, I guess. The door fought me, inexorably squeezing itself closed. '*Ow*,' I yelled, the doorknob burning my hands in that weird way that only ice can do.

Jay's hands closed around mine, and suddenly the door's trajectory was reversed. Inch by inch, we prised it open until Jay could get a foot in between it and the doorjamb.

There was no stopping him after that. He dragged the reluctant door open by sheer brute force, face thunderous, and finished the process off by way of a couple of rather savage kicks. 'You can let go,' he said, and dragged my hands away from the doorknob.

I relinquished it gratefully. Jay, standing squarely in the way of the door, wouldn't let me go in until he'd turned my hands palm-up and checked them over.

'Hurts?' he asked.

I twitched my fingers. 'Ow,' I confirmed.

He glanced again at the door, and the thunderous look returned. Was he angry with it for burning my hands? 'I've nothing to say in defence of the door's conduct,' I offered.

'But in fairness, it was me who grabbed the handle like an idiot.'

Jay released me. 'Whatever's out here better be worth it.'

At first glance, it didn't look like it. Stepping from Torvaston's spectacular bedchamber into his hidden rooms was like going from a palace into a monastery. We beheld a simple scholar's cell, white-walled, with an unpolished oaken floor and a single desk — the high-backed kind, once commonly used in cloister libraries.

I hastened eagerly towards that desk, my injury forgotten.

But only disappointment awaited me there. The desk was bare. No ancient quill-pen did I see, lying where Torvaston (presumably) had left it before he died. No stone inkwell sat waiting, filled with peculiarly fresh ink.

No books, scrolls or diaries lay open and inviting, filled with ancient secrets for Val to pore over.

'I don't understand,' I said, searching in vain for signs of something interesting in that room. 'Why was this place hidden and protected, if there's nothing here?'

'Well.' Jay paced back and forth, his dark eyes scanning every inch of the walls and floor. 'If the room itself was hidden and protected, does it not stand to reason that its contents might be as well?'

Hmm.

I devoted myself to a close scrutiny of the desk. I patted it all over with my hands, searching for signs of a hidden drawer. I knocked upon its panels, hoping for hollow sounds suggestive of a secret compartment.

Nothing.

'What is it that you are doing?' came Earl Evemer's voice all of a sudden, and he sounded every inch an aristocrat. Grave, pompous, disapproving.

'Looking for something significant,' I answered, without stopping what I was doing. Having got this far, we weren't stopping just because Luan wanted to treat Torvaston's personal effects as religious relics.

'Be *careful*,' he snapped, as I knocked a little too hard on the heavy oak wood and made it rattle a bit.

'I could set fire to this thing and it would be virtually untouched,' I said, with faint annoyance. 'They're built to withstand the apocalypse, and this one no doubt has heavy magickal wards as well.'

Luan began to look like a harassed parent with two exhaustingly wayward offspring. 'I begin to think—' he said, but whatever he had begun to think was destined to remain forever unknown, for Jay's cry of triumph interrupted him.

I looked up. Jay stood face-to-face with a plain, white-washed expanse of wall. He had his fingers in something. As I watched, he peeled back a section of the wall like it was wallpaper.

Which it wasn't. I felt a surge of magick from his corner of the room; he was stripping away glamours like they were pasted on with glue.

I made a mental note to ask him how he'd done that, later.

Behind the glamoured wall, another door lay concealed, but this one was tiny — about two feet square, and positioned about seven feet off the floor.

Over Jay's head, and well over mine.

'I need a box to stand on, or something,' said Jay, breathless with excitement, because above his head the door — crystalline and sparkling with magick — was slowly opening.

'Allow me,' said Luan severely. Before either of us could interfere, he reached up with ease and extracted the contents of the glamoured space in the wall.

My librarian's heart beat quick, for it was a scroll, and a good one, too. Wide and fat, it contained a great deal of rolled-up parchment. It practically glowed with promise, but that might just have been my fevered imagination.

I stopped breathing as Luan slowly, carefully unrolled it.

'These are plans,' he said, in the hushed voice of awe.

'Tell me they're for the Heart,' I blurted.

He didn't so much as glance at me, his gaze glued to the parchment. 'I... I believe that is exactly what they are.'

14

I PELTED TOWARDS JAY and Luan, dying for a glimpse of the scroll for myself. Plans for the Heart of Hyndorin! A paint-by-numbers how-to I could take back to Mandridore, from which they could build their very own magickal regulator.

Farringale would be saved.

The magick of the sixth Britain would be saved.

We'd done it.

But as I approached, Luan turned away from me, hiding the drawings behind his very broad back. 'Hey,' I objected. He'd pushed Jay out, too, and stood hogging all that delicious arcane knowledge for himself.

'This must be destroyed,' he said.

My jaw dropped. 'What?' I squeaked.

'For the same reason that His Majesty destroyed the Heart itself.' Luan began rolling up the scroll again, handling it with exquisite care. I wondered why he bothered, if he was just going to burn it or something. 'If it should fall into the wrong hands...'

Hard to argue with that. If it fell into the wrong hands, the consequences could be bad.

Well, so what. The same went for literally every good thing ever known to man or beast. Or troll.

'You can't destroy it,' I said, exchanging a look of pure horror with Jay. 'It's too important for that.'

'Precisely,' said Luan, unmoved.

'Torvaston left this here on purpose,' I said. 'He went to a lot of trouble to leave a trail to it, too. Why did he do that, if someone wasn't supposed to follow it someday?'

Luan hesitated, but only briefly. 'His Majesty had not, at that time, beheld modern Vale.'

'No, but he saw it coming. That's why he destroyed the original. But he still thought it worthwhile to leave this here for us.'

Luan said nothing.

'He knew magick would decline in our world,' I said. 'His writings suggest it. He left the keys to get in here in *our* Britain, and I think that's because he left this here for us. We were supposed to find it someday, and use it. To mend the damage done to Farringale. To reverse the decline of magick. To fix things, Luan! Don't take that from us. Please. We have to get this back to Their Majesties at Mandridore. They have a right to it, as Torvaston's heirs.'

Luan looked at me. Instead of the anger or disapproval or even fear I had expected to see in his face, I saw profound sadness. 'This was once the grandest, the most marvellous of all the Enclaves of Britain,' he said. 'Without contest or question. It was a place of... pure wonder. All that's gone now.'

'No,' I said. 'It's still a place of pure wonder. We've seen nothing like it.'

He shook his head. 'It is nothing to compare to its heights. Nothing at all. And that is because of the Heart. The acrimony that it caused, the conflicts, the destruction...'

'The Heart may be the reason for Hyndorin's downfall,' I said. 'But it was also the power behind its days of glory. Without the Heart, neither the one nor the other could ever have happened. Luan, if you destroy this, you ensure that neither your Britain nor mine will ever see its like again.'

'Especially ours,' put in Jay.

I gave him a moment to think. We were getting somewhere, I could see it.

Then I said, 'This is what His Majesty wanted.'

Luan hesitated, and sighed — and offered the scroll to me.

I grabbed it quick, with both hands, before he could change his mind. 'Thank you,' I said. 'Future generations will worship at the shrine of you.'

Jay frowned at me.

Right. Poor taste.

Hastily, I tucked the precious scroll into my shoulder-bag. I wanted it out of Luan's sight, before he could work himself back around to another fit of opposition. Out of sight, out of mind?

Also, I wanted Mr. Mauf and Mr. Scroll to get acquainted. I didn't yet know what Mauf had contrived to absorb down in that old workshop, but if he compared whatever he'd got with the contents of the new scroll, the results might be quite interesting.

Time for a speedy subject change. 'About Pup,' I said to Jay. 'I don't see her up here. Whereabouts did you leave her?'

'Silver stores,' he said. 'Which are...' he looked blank, and shrugged. 'Somewhere else. All this voluntary/involuntary teleporting has me confused.'

I directed a hopeful look at Luan.

'Allow me to be quite clear,' he said, and the disapproving tone was back. 'You will not be leaving here with that scroll, *and* our stores of Silver.'

'We have not the slightest wish to,' I assured him, which was a total lie, because the second I set eyes on that "gigantic pile" of fabulously valuable Silver I knew I would want every single scrap of it. 'All we want is to retrieve Pup, and get out of your hair.'

'My hair?'

Oops. 'Just an expression.'

'We're going home,' Jay supplied.

'Well, they're going home,' I amended.

'You are staying?' said Luan, swift with suspicion.

'I suppose so.'

'Where?'

'I... don't know.' The prospect of being left behind while Jay and Alban and Em went home sent the bottom dropping out of my stomach. Where would I go? What would I do, stranded in the fifth Britain by myself?

'We aren't leaving without you,' said Jay firmly, and I could almost have kissed him for that, except that it would never do.

'You have to,' I retorted. 'Someone's got to get this scroll to Mandridore, and quickly.'

'Then first we need to fix you.'

Fix me, like I was a broken refrigerator. Malfunctioning gadgetry, just see the repairman and all will be well.

I realised I was gazing at Jay with the Eyes of Hope, and hastily composed myself. 'Do you think it's possible?'

'Ves. If there's one thing I've learned from hanging around with you, it's that every gods-damned insane thing imaginable is probably possible, if you can manage to be batshit crazy enough.'

My turn of phrase was rubbing off on Jay. 'Are we batshit crazy enough?'

'Always.'

My eyes filled momentarily with tears, rather to my shame. Sensible, unflappable, by-the-book Jay was volunteering to be a total madman for my sake.

My corrupting influence knew no bounds.

Jay gave a slight cough, and added, 'Of course, we could use a little help.' He was looking at Luan as he said it, the cheek. As though we hadn't already complicated the poor Earl's day enough.

Luan, unfortunately, looked nonplussed.

'I have an idea,' I said. 'Magickal Silver absorbs magick, right? So how about you throw me head-first into that gigantic pile of yours and see how much of me comes out.'

Jay looked appalled.

'It'll be okay,' I said, with a reassuring smile. 'I'm pretty sure I'll still have arms, legs and a head.'

'No,' said Luan. 'I am sorry, but there is no known way to reverse the effects you refer to.'

I swallowed, for once in my life struck speechless. *No way to reverse the effects.* I was stuck forever. I would never see

Home again. I'd have to spend the rest of my life living in Vale, just to be comfortable.

Only iron will kept me from bursting into tears and sobbing like a five-year-old all over Jay's shirt.

Jay stared at me.

I can't absolutely guarantee that my lip didn't quiver, or that I didn't look back at him with the lost look of a stray puppy.

I *tried* to be dignified, but news like that tends to cut a person off at the knees.

'There has to be a way,' Jay said, jaw set. 'If we have to move a gods-damned mountain to get Ves home, we'll do it.'

'Jay—' I began.

He cut me off. 'Do you think Alban or Em wouldn't say the same? We are not leaving without you.' He enunciated the last six words clearly and with emphasis; clearly comprehensible, even for an idiot like me.

I took a shaky breath, and nodded. 'Luan. You mentioned that some of you leave Hyndorin on occasion, but you implied that it wasn't in order to visit another magick-drenched location, such as Vale.'

'We go shopping,' he said, with a twinkle. 'Once in a while.'

'In places of lesser magickal impact?'

'Yes. Enclaves as — what did you call it? — *magick-drenched* as Hyndorin and Vale are not common, even in this Britain.'

'How do you manage it, then? For if you live here with ease, you must be as magick-drowned as I am.' I hoped. Either that or they were just used to dosing themselves with powdered unicorn horn every six hours.

Somehow I didn't think that was it. Hundreds of years had passed. Generation after generation had lived here, and stayed here, even when they had little reason to remain.

'The arts relating to the creatures known as Familiars,' said Luan. 'Are they still known about, in your Britain?'

'No,' I said. 'Well, yes. But it is rarely practiced, and bordering upon illegal, because we're stupid about it.' That was roughly what Miranda had said.

'A deep bond with a suitable creature can be of great use,' said Luan. 'But such a bond should not be lightly entered into, for it is permanent, and it will change you.'

'Change me?' I echoed dumbly. I mean, I wanted to be changed, at this point, but that was vague.

'A Familiar may enhance its bonded partner's magick, or alternatively it may lessen it,' said Luan. 'This is because, once fully bonded with a Familiar, its magick becomes yours, and vice versa. The bond is one of shared magick, and it is absolute.'

So if I were overflowing with too much of it, I could pool my magick with my Familiar, reducing the excess upon myself and strengthening my beast. Or, the other way around.

'But,' cautioned Luan. 'It is no easy thing to arrange. Understand that an ordinary domestic cat or dog, or any creature commonly kept as a pet, will not serve. Even the more common of the magickal breeds will not do.'

'Not Pup, then?' asked Jay.

Luan shook his head. 'A nose-for-gold, however talent-ed, has not the depths of magick necessary to serve well as a Familiar. I do not believe I have ever heard of such a bond being formed.'

I swallowed, my throat suddenly dry. 'How about... a unicorn?'

I waited, crossing my fingers behind my back.

Luan paused in thought. 'Perhaps,' he allowed. 'Some are much diminished now. Those you will have observed at Vale, for example, are little better than cattle, poor crea-tures.'

'But a unicorn of royal lines?' said Jay, anticipating my line of thought.

'Royal lines?' said Luan, with a curious tilt of his head. 'Is that what they are calling them now?'

'Apparently. Could such a unicorn function as a Famil-iar?'

'Indeed, yes,' said Luan, and I could have cried with relief. 'One of my sisters has such a Familiar.'

Milady's words floated through my mind. *And, Ves, if you can contrive to take your unicorn companion along, you may also find that a useful measure.*

Ha. To say the least. Had she known how useful, when she'd said those words, and in what way? Or was it just a hunch?

Thank you, Milady, I told her in my thoughts. Thanks to her foresight, however it worked, I might actually get the chance to say that to her in person sometime soon.

'Next question,' I said. 'Um. How does one go about bonding with a Familiar?'

15

'You cannot simply bond with a Familiar at your own convenience,' said Luan severely. 'A living, magickal beast is not an artefact to pick up and drop at will, or a toy to play with whenever the mood takes you.'

'I know that,' I said, as patiently as I could. Honestly, he sounded like Miranda.

'It takes months, and in some cases years, to forge a trusting relationship with a suitable animal,' continued Luan.

'No problem there,' I said. 'Addie and I have been going strong for a decade.'

That gave him pause, and a little of the disapproval smoothed out of his features. 'Then, if the creature is willing, you may create a soul-bond via a magickal binding. It is common to employ a catalyst to complete this process.'

'A binding?' I said. 'That sounds uncomfortably like the griffins and unicorns up at Vale.'

'No. There are great differences. For one, it is not possible to force such a bond upon any creature. They may reject it at any time, and many do. For another, it is a link that goes both ways. You are not binding a unicorn into your personal service, as though it were some manner of slave. You will be at your Familiar's service, too.'

'And it is permanent, you said?' asked Jay.

'Naturally. Such a bond may only be severed by the death of one or both parties.'

I began to understand why Familiar-bonding was bordering upon banned in our Britain. Serious business.

Addie was no low-level magickal beastie. Unicorns were among the most powerful of creatures, surpassed only by the likes of dragons and griffins. I thought back to what Miranda had said. *People try to take on creatures of far greater magickal potency than they can handle. The beast suffers, and the owner probably ends up as mincemeat.*

Could I handle a unicorn? Or would I hurt Addie, and wind up as mincemeat?

Course, the link worked both ways, and I was presently a magickal powerhouse. Could Addie handle *me*?

'And this is why we needed Miranda,' I said to Jay, with a rueful smile. I'd resented Milady's insistence on that particular point, but she'd been right. Again.

'Right. We find Miranda and we make this happen,' said Jay.

'First, though, we retrieve Pup.'

WE FOUND MY DISGRACEFUL Goodie Two-Shoes (hah) lying upside-down atop the Hyndorin Silver stash, belly turned up, paws limp, and a sublime grin upon her tiny houndy face. 'Drunk on treasure,' I said, shaking my head. 'That's our Pup.'

'She looks like a felled dandelion,' said Jay.

'A dandelion of unusual size.'

The Silver storeroom was situated not far from Torvaston's chambers, which I thought was likely not a coincidence. Jay had seen a flash of yellow fur as Pup whisked past, and followed her there.

I'd expected a stout room with a stout door and lots of security, but the Silver Stash had none of those things. The place was more of a spacious alcove, decorated with mosaic tiles and gilding and all that jazz, and the Silver occupied a depression in the floor. It shone softly, moon-pale, and seemed piled there more as a decoration in its own right.

'Won't somebody steal it, if you leave it out in the open like this?' I said to Luan.

He looked oddly at me. 'Somebody who?'

I was forgetting the layer upon layer of magick and illusion which protected their hideout from outside intruders. Nobody had penetrated all that guff in many a long year, so fair enough. And apparently they didn't have a problem with their own citizens making off with the loot, for it was all still here.

I nudged one of Pup's splayed-out paws with my toe, and she woke with a start.

'Come on,' I told her, looking meaningfully at the door. 'Fun's over.'

Pup whined, and flattened her ears.

'I know, life is unspeakably hard. But you still can't waltz off with all of Hyndorin's worldly goods.'

She slunk down off her personal Treasure Mountain, and trailed over to me, tail drooping.

I felt like the worst person alive.

'I'll get you something shiny when we get home,' I promised her, and patted her ears.

No response.

'Parenting,' said Jay. 'It'll break your heart.'

I stuck my tongue out at him. 'We're going,' I informed them both, and checked to make sure I still had Torvaston's scroll of exciting plans, plus Mauf. 'My lord Evemer.

We thank you most heartily for your time and assistance, for ourselves and also on behalf of Their Majesties at Mandridore.'

Luan bowed. 'It is a pleasure to be of service to Their Majesties,' he said, without conviction. Still harbouring doubts, was he? I couldn't blame him, but that was too bad. No one's life work ever did anyone any good gathering dust in a vault.

I pictured how delighted the Majesties in question were going to be, when we came back with the plans. And how pleased and interested Alban would be, when we showed them to him. How incredible Farringale would become, once released from the curse of the ortherex. The entire troll nation would be reunited with this vital piece of their magickal heritage. The entirety of our Britain could look forward to a stronger, more magickal future.

I've never done anything so important, or so satisfying, in my life.

When we left the tower and stepped out into what was left of the afternoon's summery sunshine, I was walking on air.

I didn't come down, even when we encountered Wyr on the doorstep and he was still a tree. If anything, he was settling in to his new, leafier life, for his rather formless shape of before had acquired some refinements. 'He's a chestnut,' I informed Jay, inspecting the Wyr-leaves. 'I think.'

Jay shook his head. 'He's nothing I recognise. He's his own, unique kind of tree. A Wyr-tree.'

'Are we leaving him like this?'

'Do you have any idea how to change him back?'

I did not.

I *did* try, honest. As it turns out, you can give a Ves as much power as you like, but if she has no idea what to do with it, then nothing can help her.

'He likes being a tree,' I decided at last. 'That's the only possible explanation.'

'Nothing to do with ignorance or ineptitude on the part of the enchanter,' said Jay.

'Nothing whatsoever.'

'If you're finished failing at reverse transmogrification, shall we go find the others?' He stepped onto the lift-stone and I followed, pretending not to notice as Pup performed a second set of, er, ablutions around Wyr's roots.

Hey, he was in no condition to mind.

'Right, where did we leave the others?' I said, as we arrived back at the base of the rocky promontory. A glance up revealed that it was a mountain again, or so it appeared; Torvaston's spectacular tower was gone from my sight.

I experienced a brief stab of regret. I may have had no interest in remaining in the Hyndorin Enclave forever, but in all probability I would never see that tower again.

Anyway. 'Thataway,' I said, waving an arm in what I imagined to be Alban's general direction.

'No, I don't think that was one of them,' said Jay, glancing about in that keen-eyed way he had when he was getting his bearings. He set off after a moment, and Pup and I trailed after him.

Ten minutes later, though, we'd walked and walked without coming across anybody at all. 'Who are we looking for just now?' I called to Jay.

'Em was out here,' he said with a frown.

'Are you sure?'

'Positive.' Was that a trace of irritation I detected? Fair enough, if it was. Who was I to question Jay's sense of direction?

But after another five minutes, I could see that Jay, too, was beginning to doubt. 'Let's try for Alban,' he said, and changed direction.

I smothered my unease. I could have sworn we had passed right through the glade in which we had previously left Emellana; I'd seen a pair of withered orchard trees that looked familiar. But what did I know? I never could remember very well what I had or hadn't seen. I was probably wrong.

But for Jay and I both to be so vague was not at all common, and when we failed to find Alban either, I began to feel worried.

'This is odd,' said Jay, stopping. 'This is where Alban was standing. I could swear to it.'

'Something's going on,' I said. I wouldn't doubt Jay twice. He had proved the superiority of his navigational skills time and time again.

'It might be nothing,' Jay said. 'After all, once we were inside the tower they didn't need to stay put. They probably got bored of standing in the same spot, and went off somewhere.'

'Likely true, but where? Surely they'd gather somewhere near where we were likely to come out.'

'That would make sense,' said Jay.

'Where else would they go? There isn't anything else here.' Except natural beauty, but unless the three of them had developed a sudden passion for any particular tree or hillock, I couldn't see why they would have wandered off.

My sense of foreboding deepened.

'Right,' said Jay. 'They obviously aren't where we left them, and just as obviously did not choose to wait near the tower. So. Where else could they be?'

'Somewhere we have yet to explore,' I said. 'It isn't an especially large valley. Where haven't we been?'

Jay took off without comment, and I hurried to catch up. He walked much faster this time, driven by the same alarm I felt. *It's probably nothing,* I told myself again, but we would both of us be much more comfortable when the mystery was solved and we were reunited with our friends. They were probably sunbathing on a nice rock somewhere, feasting upon orchard fruits that looked like apples but smelled like cherries.

I kept my eyes peeled (what a disgusting saying) and my ears open (bizarre: who closes their ears?), but nothing met my searching gaze but more verdure, and I heard only stray birdsong, and the rustling of tall grass in the breeze.

I ached to hear Alban's voice. Just one little word would do.

'We've lost them,' I moaned after a while. 'The Court lent us one of their most powerful practitioners *and* the heir to the throne, and we've lost them.'

'Not forgetting Miranda,' said Jay. I'd still love to forget Miranda more often if I could, but not like this.

It was then that Pup's hunting instincts kicked in. Throughout our fruitless search, she had ambled along at my heels, apparently uninterested in anything going on around her. Still sulking about the Silver Stash, I'd thought. But she got a whiff of something electrifying, and abruptly took off at a full gallop.

I exchanged a look with Jay, and we broke into a run, pounding through the grass after her.

'It's nothing,' I panted after a while, as we ran and ran and encountered only more grassy meadow. 'Pup's just having one of her mad moments—'

I stopped dead and shut my stupid mouth, for the view changed. An instant before, I'd seen only an expanse of tall grass dotted with wildflowers, stretching as far as the horizon.

Then, between one step and the next, a building loomed out of the empty air. A familiar building.

'Jay,' I whispered. 'What the giddy gods is Ashdown Castle doing here?'

16

'By the looks of it, Ashdown Castle is lying in wait,' said Jay.

'For us,' I groaned. 'This is what Alban meant, when he said Ancestria Magicka had some kind of a spy at Court. They knew we were headed out here.'

'And they hoped we would be coming out with something priceless.'

'Which we are.'

'We can't let them get hold of those plans,' said Jay.

'But that's why they're here. And they've got Alban and Emellana and Mir. They must do. And they're waiting for us to walk right into the trap, which we are presently in the process of doing.'

'Hostage situation?' said Jay.

'Right. They'll try to trade our friends for our loot. And ordinarily I wouldn't hesitate to go for a trade like that, but this is no ordinary loot.' I backed up until Ashdown Castle disappeared from sight, then dumped my bag on the floor and crouched over it, rummaging through the contents. 'Mauf, speak,' I said, locating my precious book at the bottom. 'Tell me you've got a grip on that scroll.'

'I have done my best, madam.'

That would have to be enough. 'The fate of the world rests in your hands,' I informed Mauf as I drew out the scroll.

'Regrettably, I have no hands,' Mauf pointed out.

'Your capable pages, then,' I said, but absently, for I was busy eyeballing the scroll. 'Or, maybe not entirely. Jay, got your phone handy?' I'd let mine fall into the depths of my jumbled bag of paraphernalia, and it could take way too long to find it.

Jay however whipped his out in seconds, and was already snapping pics the moment I had the scroll unrolled. 'But this isn't helpful,' he objected. 'Keeping our own copies is good. Giving Ancestria Magicka the original is unthinkable.'

'I know.' My hands trembled as I gripped the aged vellum of that priceless scroll, and I had to take a moment to get a grip on myself. What I was about to do went as badly against the grain as defacing library books, or torching Orlando's lab.

It took very little power, in the end. I watched sadly as the inked lines of Torvaston's elaborate drawings began to fade.

'Ves, no—' Jay began, but it was already too late. I held a blank sheet of parchment in my hands. The original plans for the Heart of Hyndorin were gone forever.

Quickly, I rolled the scroll back up and secured it, then placed it back into the bag with Mauf. 'Guard that phone with your life,' I told Jay, and without speaking he zipped it into an inside pocket in his jacket.

'Right,' I said, straightening up. 'It's time for an exciting game of chance. Are you ready?'

'You're going to bluff your way through a hostage exchange?' Jay said.

'Do you have a better idea?'

Jay looked at me like I'd grown a second head. Again. I felt a twinge of disappointment, for it had been a while since he'd looked at me with such naked horror. I'd thought I was making some progress in his esteem.

Well. I *had* just callously erased the contents of a priceless academic artefact. And if we didn't play our collective cards right, we'd either get our friends back but lose all trace of the plans, or we'd lose the lot. Including Alban, Em and Mir.

I tried not to think that way. Ancestria Magicka may be thoroughly unscrupulous, but they'd yet to show signs of murderous tendencies.

Still, the stakes were high. Dangerously high.

'Are you with me or not?' I said, skipping over the soothing platitudes. I wanted Jay to trust me, but we didn't have time for long, self-justifying conversations just then.

'Lead on,' said Jay briefly, without the professions of faith and loyalty I was hoping for.

Oh well. When I set off in the direction of Ashdown Castle, Jay came with me, and that was the important part.

'Are we just going to walk right up to the door?' said Jay a moment later, as we approached the castle in full view of the windows.

'Why not? They knew we'd come. They are waiting for us.'

'It doesn't seem right. No sneaking? None?'

'What would be the point? It's very hard to sneak past a castleful of people on high alert, looking specifically for *you*. Anyway, I want them to think they've won. That's the whole point.'

'Right.' I detected more than a trace of doubt in the word, but Jay strode on beside me. 'Where did Pup go?' he said.

'That... is a very good question.' I'd momentarily forgotten about Pup's headlong gallop, while I was grappling with the morality of erasing an irreplaceable scroll versus leaving my friends to an unknown fate. What had Goodie been haring towards?

Then something barrelled into me, something *heavy*, and knocked me flat. 'Ves!' said a familiar voice. 'Don't go in there!'

'Zar?' I pushed her off me, and tried to sit up, but she shoved me back down again. She had contrived to do the same to Jay, and we all three lay prone in the grass.

Something tickled my ankle. When I lifted my head to investigate, I beheld a bundle of tufty yellow fur and an enormous nose, the latter in pursuit of an enchanting scent relating to my left foot.

Ah. Pup had caught a whiff of Zareen on the wind, and boldly tracked her down.

'Zar,' I said again. 'What the dickens are you doing here?'

'Same as you,' she said. 'I was drawn here by wicked, deceitful arts, courtesy of our best friends Ancestria Magicka.' She spoke with a vicious bitterness most out of character for her, and when I looked at her I beheld her usually calm face creased into a dark scowl. Her green-streaked hair was in a state of wild disorder; deep shadows under her eyes proclaimed her exhaustion; and she was pasty-pale, which wasn't usual for her either. She'd had a hard week, clearly. But she was alive.

I felt a knot of tension ease somewhere inside. I'd been worried about Zareen for some time, but with no idea where she had ended up and no way to follow, I hadn't been able to do anything about it. 'What happened to you?' I said, but when I tried to sit up she pushed me back down again.

'Ves, you can't let them know you're here. That's what they *want*. They're waiting for you.'

'We know.'

She blinked. 'Then what the hell are you doing?'

'Tell you in a minute. First, fill us in.'

She sighed, and let her head fall back into the grass. 'George and I were working on those trapped spirits in the castle, trying to calm them down. Get them together. Build them up for one last jump, to a permanent new location for the castle. Then we were going to release them.'

'I remember that part,' I said. 'No joy?'

'Actually, we were doing pretty well. Until Fenella Eff-ing Beaumont showed up, with her miserable crowd of cronies. Apparently they remembered a few things.'

'Ah. Then Melmidoc happened?'

'Right. He got pissed, and banished the entire castle to the worst Britain *ever*, do not go there, I am not kidding. The *entire* castle, Ves, with me and George in it, and Fenella and co as well.' She paused for an instant, then contin-ued, 'George declared himself *"done"* with being dragged around after me, and the *"stupid"* stuff we were doing, and abased himself before Fenella, who graciously welcomed him back into the fold. Which left me, hiding in the walls while the lot of them played hunt-the-chicken, and George tried to coax me to throw in my lot with *them.*'

That explained both her exhaustion and her anger. I sensed a lengthy rant pending, but Zar got a grip on herself. 'Long story short,' she said. 'It was some days before the castle could return to the fifth. In that time, I heard a few snatches of conversation between Fenella and some of her ratty disciples. They knew far too much about what you were doing, Ves. They probably knew about your current mission before you did. They had a plan to get hold of a certain scroll-case, which fell through; I didn't catch why. The new plan was to lie low for a while, let you do the work while imagining yourselves unopposed, then swoop in at the end and swipe the goods.'

'Which is where we're at,' said Jay, and gestured at the castle. 'Swooping in progress.'

'Yes, but you don't have to just walk in there like a pair of idiots! Why do you think I risked discovery, in order to wait here for you?'

I patted her arm. 'It was brilliant of you, Zar, and we're both grateful and admiring. But they have Alban, and Miranda, and Emellana.'

'Emellana. That the troll lady with the purple shirt?'

'Right.'

'Mm. That wasn't anticipated, I think. Did you *have* to leave three associates on the outside, standing around by themselves, just waiting to be kidnapped? They were sitting ducks.'

'Actually yes, it was necessary. We would have much preferred to take them with us.'

'Well, I hope whatever you got was worth it. They're all in there, and it won't be easy to get them out.'

'Yes, it will. We just have to do whatever they want.' With which words, I stood up again, resisting Zareen's attempts to render me prone, and dusted grass seeds off my clothes. 'Which I intend to do without delay.'

'You can't.' Zareen stared at me, appalled. 'I don't have a clear idea what you two got a hold of, except that it's game-changing.'

'World-changing,' I said, nodding. 'Don't worry. I have a plan.'

Zareen rolled her eyes.

'She's going to bluff,' said Jay.

'*Bluff?*' repeated Zareen.

'The timing will be tight,' I said. 'We need to make the trade, then get the lot of us out of there before they discover our sneaky double-cross.'

Zareen stared at Jay, as if to say, *are you going along with this madness?*

Jay shrugged. He'd gained his feet, too, and now fell in beside me. 'Onward, captain.'

Zareen groaned, and said distinctly, '*Fuck* my life.'

'It's a good life,' I said, smiling. 'It may not feel like it right now, but someday you'll remember what food and sleep and friendship are like, and it'll be okay again.' I held out my hand to her, and with another muttered curse she grasped it, and permitted herself to be hauled up. 'How long has the castle been lurking out here?'

'A couple of days.'

'Right. Let's go.' We set off towards Ashdown Castle, me trying to walk like a woman of confidence and not like a woman whose legs felt like jelly and whose guts were churning with unease. *What if I was wrong?*

No time to worry about that now. I lifted my chin, and sailed towards the castle like I'd never heard the words *reckless, mission-wrecking insanity* in my life.

Some distance still lay between us and the front door. As we crossed it, walking at a brisk but leisurely pace, I had ample opportunity to observe the effects of repeated teleportation upon the crumbling old castle. It had been in poor shape to begin with, due to centuries of insufficient care. Three or four jumps across worlds had not been good for it. Some of its chimneys were gone, tumbled into pieces; windows were a mess of broken glass and warped leading; holes had opened up in the walls, where its mortar had crumbled and brown bricks had fallen away. A building on its last legs, so to speak. It wouldn't be long before the walls collapsed and ceilings caved in.

I tightened my resolve. Ancestria Magicka had no respect for history, magickal or otherwise. No doubt they would do their utmost to justify themselves, and cajole us into taking their side. They wouldn't receive an ounce of sympathy from me.

Throughout that nerve-wracking stroll, I had the prickly feeling of eyes upon me. Lots of eyes. And here came the proof, for as we neared the great oaken doors, they swung slowly open.

Fenella Beaumont herself stood upon the threshold, smiling graciously at us.

'Welcome, Miss Vesper, Mr. Patel,' she said smoothly. 'And Miss Dalir. How charming of you to join us at last.'

Zareen's scowl deepened. Before she could say anything, I cut in. 'Ms. Beaumont. How about we glide past the chit-chat, and get down to business? We're here to retrieve our friends.'

'Do you know, I thought you might be?' Her smile widened, and so did the doors. 'Do come in. They await you in the long drawing-room.'

Invoking my Nerves of Steel, I followed Fenella Beaumont into the depths of enemy territory, Jay and Zareen and Pup right behind me.

17

THE LAST TIME I'D seen Fenella Beaumont, she had been wearing a flashy designer evening-gown and too many diamonds. She'd hosted a massive party for a large group of magickal invitees — including us — in this very castle, specifically for the purpose of breaking the news about the fifth Britain. Jay and Zareen and the Baron and I had wrecked her little coup, which hadn't exactly made us popular with her.

Her smiling friendliness unnerved me. So angry had she been about our interference, she'd taken an axe to poor Millie's doors and windows. Now she welcomed us to her ancestral castle with impeccable manners and a smooth smile — the same castle Zareen had lately endeavoured to wrest from her entirely, with the help of George Mercer, supposedly one of her own employees. Was her friendliness purely because we had the answer to all her wildest magickal dreams in our possession? Fenella's stated ambition was to revive magick in our own Britain, no doubt for nefarious purposes of her own. Torvaston's invention would be as exciting to her as it was to us.

Still, I would have expected at least a genteel insult or two, delivered through that smiling mouth. Her elegant self-possession was out of character for a woman capable of hacking through solid oak doors in a fit of temper, and her air of gracious welcome was over the top.

And her captives now included all the people responsible for the collapse of her carefully-nurtured plans.

'I do believe we're in for a double crossing,' I murmured to Jay and Zareen, as we followed Fenella through Ashdown Castle's great hall.

Jay agreed. 'I don't think it's going to be as simple as hand over the scroll and high-tail it out of here.'

Zareen's only response was a black look of pure hatred. I wondered briefly what had passed between them during the days they'd been stranded in some other Britain together, and decided not to enquire.

'You okay, Zar?' I said.

'No,' she said shortly.

Fair enough.

Mission Objective: Retrieve Alban, Emellana and Miranda from Fenella Beaumont's clutches, preferably without handing over any part whatsoever of Torvaston's ancient research, then fly like bats out of hell. *Before* any of us went stark raving bonkers (again), or did anything we might regret; and without falling prey to any of Ms. Beaumont's inevitable schemes for our downfall.

Easy.

The long drawing-room turned out to be a vision in sage-coloured silk and brocade, and in surprisingly good shape considering the tumbling-down state of the castle. It had the pristine, polished look of recent refurbishment, though since the room's historic character had been meticulously preserved, it had to have been expensive. Very expensive.

Was the entire castle scheduled for a similar upgrade? The money it would take to restore Ashdown to its original condition would run into breath-taking sums, and I wondered, once again, where Ancestria Magicka's cash came from. The Beaumont family had sold the castle to the corporation, which Fenella claimed to have founded. But that sale had been made because the family was virtually destitute. Either Fenella had somehow made eye-watering sums of money while she'd been somewhere off the radar (and if so I seriously wanted to know how); or they had an incredibly wealthy backer somewhere. We still didn't know who that might be.

'Nice paint job,' I said lightly as we walked in. 'Must've cost a bit.' I scanned the room as I spoke. Alban stood near the fireplace, leaning one arm against the mantelpiece. He looked up at the sound of my voice, and smiled, but there was tension in every line of his body, and the smile was strained and forced. Emellana sat in a huge armchair a few feet away, ostensibly her usual serene self, though with a watchfulness about her that I hadn't before seen. She looked at me without smiling, and I could not read what might be going on in her mind. Both of them looked oddly docile, considering their predicament. Either they were under some kind of enchantment courtesy of Fenella, or they were planning something, and waiting for the right moment to strike. Which was probably our arrival.

Things could get interesting, pretty soon.

Miranda stood by the window, looking thunderous. She glanced at me, and looked away, but not before I'd got a glimpse of the terror that lay behind her rage. Hardly surprising either. She'd lately betrayed the Society in favour of Ancestria Magicka, then betrayed Ancestria Magicka in order to help the Society, and now she was surrounded by representatives of both. Not an enviable position to be in.

Her own fault. I hardened my heart, at least for the present, and set that matter aside. We would get her out. What she did after that would be up to her.

'It cost *quite* a bit,' said Fenella drily, and waved a hand, indicating the glittering contents of her drawing-room as though she was personally responsible for the lot. 'Like what you see?'

Actually, I did. The room was a vision of possibility. All the castles and great houses of Britain could look like this, if only there was money enough. But there never was. Most of them mouldered away under minimal maintenance, and too many fell into ruin. 'It's magnificent,' I said, with total honesty.

She smirked. 'What if I told you it wasn't money that did this? Or, not *only* money.'

'Then what was it?'

'Magick.' She stood between me and her hostages, watching me like some kind of widow spider. She was more casually dressed than she'd been the last time we had met, in a blouse and trousers, her silvery hair caught up in a simple knot. But she still reeked of money, and she had the predatory air to match.

'So it's illusion?' I said, disappointed. Fakery was of little practical use.

'No. Everything that you see here is real.'

'I'm confused. You used magick to reupholster some chairs...? I suppose, if you've got the manpower—'

'You aren't thinking, Ves.' Fenella cut me off.

'Don't call me Ves,' I snapped.

'Ves,' said Alban. 'They've used magick to regenerate everything in this room.'

'*Regenerate*?'

He met my eyes, and nodded. He didn't have to say anything else. My mind was already reeling.

See, regenerating damaged or decayed objects — or creatures — is one of the many arts we've just about lost. *If* it ever existed within the realms of possibility at all, and there are multiple schools of thought on that topic. It's why the Society employs ordinary doctors, like Rob, despite having some of the most powerful magickal practitioners alive on its payroll. It's why the team Miranda used to head up included a couple of veterinarians, and why we have conservators and restorers on the staff. Regenerating anything that's broken or injured would require such huge expenditures of magick, it hardly bears thinking about. I mean, can you imagine what it would *take*, to turn back the clock like that?

There simply isn't magick enough left in the world.

'That has to be a lie,' I said.

'Why?' said Fenella. 'Possibilities abound beyond the borders of our own Britain. You have seen that for yourself.'

That silenced me. I hadn't previously had any clear idea as to what Fenella and Co might want to do with Torvaston's magick-regulating project, but I'm fairly sure the word "nefarious" passed through my thoughts.

This wasn't nefarious. This was *brilliant.*

And exactly the right thing to wave in front of me, curse her.

'Well, great,' I said briskly. 'Good for you. Anyway, about our colleagues?'

'Perhaps they would like to remain here,' said Fenella, in her silkiest voice. 'Perhaps you might, too.'

'No,' said Jay briefly.

I rolled my eyes. 'Another subversion attempt? No, thank you. We are never going to be interested.'

'Oh?' said Fenella politely. 'At least one of your number has not been quite so impervious, has she?' She looked at Miranda, whose face darkened even further. 'And your own loyalties have proved to be more... flexible, than might have been expected.'

Damnit. Here was the backlash from Milady's clever, Ministry-dodging schemes. As far as Fenella knew, we had abandoned the Society some weeks ago: ostensibly in favour of founding our own rival organisation, though now we were here under the Troll Court's aegis. If we appeared unreliable, it was kind of our own fault.

'We are not interested,' I said firmly. 'We want to make the exchange and then leave. Please.'

Sadly, Fenella shook her head. 'How heart-breaking it is, to watch so remarkable a group waste your talents on such backward-thinking organisations. Bring Torvaston's work to us. Give us exclusive control over it. We will do all the beautiful, magnificent, world-changing things the Court would never countenance. And you can be a big part of that, Ves.'

'*Don't* call me Ves.'

She gave a tiny sigh, and looked at Jay, and then Zareen. Both of them shook their heads.

I felt a moment's unease. Clearly she had been having this conversation with Alban, Em and Miranda before we had arrived. They *had* refused — surely?

Of course they had. Emellana was as steady as a rock, and she'd been loyal to Mandridore all her long life through. And Alban's devotion to his adoptive parents could not be questioned, considering everything he had taken on — and given up — for them.

I wasn't sure about Miranda, and she would not meet my eye.

'You're getting Torvaston's research anyway,' I said to Fenella. 'Just as soon as you release our friends. And then we will be leaving.'

'I would prefer to have... everything.'

'That is not going to happen.'

'A pity,' said Fenella, her smile still in place. She held out her hand. 'I will take whatever it is you retrieved from that tower, then.'

'The artefact no longer exists,' I told her. 'Torvaston destroyed it. But we have his plans.' I withdrew the delicate scroll from my bag, and offered it to her. 'Release our companions, and you may take it.' *And please don't look at it now.*

She made no move to do so. 'Lovely,' she said, regarding me with narrowed eyes. 'But what a pity that the artefact no longer exists.'

'Isn't it?' I agreed. If she imagined we were hiding the thing from her, well, that was a species of red herring. Perhaps it would keep her too busy to think of inspecting the scroll.

'Well!' said Fenella, turning to smile brightly at Alban, Emellana and Miranda. 'It appears we are finished here.' She inclined her head to them, apparently in respect, and something changed. Emellana sat up, blinking, and Alban straightened.

Miranda bolted, straight for the door. Alban and Em followed. Once all my friends were safely on my side of the room, with an open door behind us, I tossed the scroll to Fenella, who caught it with a flourish.

'Perfect,' she said, and waved the scroll in dismissal. 'Delightful of you to visit. We must do this again sometime.'

Did that mean we were free to go? All of us? Without interference? I hesitated, alarms blaring in my mind. This was far too easy.

'Ves,' said Zareen. 'She's up to something. The ghosts—they're—' She broke off, crossed quickly to the nearest wall, and laid a palm against the silk wallpaper, her eyes closing.

The drawing-room door abruptly slammed shut behind us, with a resounding *boom,* and I heard the tumblers rattle as the lock turned.

Crap.

'They're what?' I said. 'Zar?'

'*George,*' she hissed, and her eyes flew open again, to settle accusingly on Fenella. 'You made him do this.'

Fenella smiled. 'George has remembered which side his bread is buttered. Shall we say that?'

'*Zar,*' I said. 'What's going on?'

'They're agitated. George is waking them up, making them—' She paused for breath. 'They're preparing to move the castle.'

Uh oh. 'Can they do that so soon?'

'George is forcing them.' These words emerged as a growl. 'You can't do this,' she said, fixing Fenella with a wrathful stare. '*This* is why none of us wants to work with you. You *use* people for your own ends, and you use them until they break. You've broken George, and you'll destroy these waymasters.'

'They are dead,' said Fenella.

'They're still *people*.' Zareen's eyes went ink-black from lid to lid, and she snarled something I couldn't decipher. She was fighting back, trying to block George's efforts to whip up the waymasters Fenella had enslaved.

She didn't have the strength for that. Not now. She'd break, too, and I wasn't at all sure if she would mend.

But I didn't know how to stop her, or George either.

18

'AND WHERE, EXACTLY, ARE we going?' Jay said coldly.

'I think we are all feeling a little homesick, are we not?' said Fenella pleasantly.

'No!' I blurted, and backed away — as if that would help. 'I can't go home yet!'

Fenella looked oddly at me.

'So the plan is to kidnap the lot of us?' said Jay disgustedly. 'We work for you, whether we will or no?'

'That remains to be seen,' said Fenella. Her hostess smile had gone; her tone was now all business. 'The fact is, I can't have you trailing back to Mandridore with the copies of that research you have no doubt made. Or perhaps with an intact artefact you'd like me to imagine no longer exists. Ancestria Magicka will bring back British magick, and no one else.'

So that was it. Pure, naked ambition. I wasn't surprised, but I was... out-manoeuvred. My mind blanked, and I couldn't think. What could we do? Run for it? I made a break for the door, but Jay was there before me.

'Locked,' he said. 'Give me a moment.'

Okay, he was going to punch one of his void-space holes in it. Fine, but then what? We might be able to subdue Fenella, but that would do us little good. We were in her territory. We wouldn't get two steps beyond the door without running into more of her agents; overpowering them would slow us down. And George could be any-where in the castle. We would never be able to find him in time to prevent him from dragging the building home.

'Quickly,' I said to Jay. Alban was at my elbow, and I caught a glimpse of Emellana's purple shirt out of the corner of my eye. If we could make it to the main doors in time—

The floor began to shake. I grabbed hold of Alban to steady myself, as my heart sank and terror turned my knees to water. This was it. The castle was moments away from a potentially fatal removal to the sixth Britain — fatal for *me*, because all the magick in me would go off like a fire-work and I'd burst like a rotten melon.

'*Ves*,' said a calm, but firm voice in my ear. Emellana. 'Help Zareen.' Her capable hands grasped my arms; she turned me to face Zar, and gave me a gentle shove.

Help Zareen with *what*? My brain gibbered helplessly, and I gulped down panic. Curse it. You'd think I could face my imminent demise with a bit more grace.

Hands steadied me again, and this time they were Alban's. 'Calm, Ves,' he said softly. 'Em is right. Zareen can't block George on her own, but with your help, perhaps she can.'

My help? I was no necromancer.

No, but I was presently functioning as a magickal power source all on my own. I was a human griffin. A magickal battery. I grabbed hold of Zareen, and tried to focus on emptying my unwanted magickal overflow into her. 'I have no idea what I'm doing,' I gasped.

Alban chuckled. 'And you'll pull it off anyway. You always do.'

But I wouldn't. Not this time. Because we were too late.

Even as I struggled to pump Zar full of all the power she'd need to wrest the castle away from George, the shaking of the floor intensified, and the walls began the slow, deep rumble of agitated brickwork. Someone screamed, a tearing noise that turned my insides to goo.

Zareen. She shrieked again, and began to babble, and I realised it wasn't *her* screaming; she was a conduit for the dead waymasters locked into the walls. She spoke — and keened — with their voices, all ten of them at once. Her face was a mask of agony. As I watched in horror, blood began to pour from the corners of her eyes.

'Shit,' I said. Never mind *my* imminent demise. Zareen was breaking into pieces before my stupid, helpless eyes.

I didn't have time to think. I just grabbed hold of her in a clumsy bearhug, my hands circling her wrists, and tried to make one entity of the two of us. We were not Zareen and Vesper, necromancer and magickal energiser bunny. We were Veseen, or Zaresper, *one uber powerful necromancer.* George was nothing to us.

The shuddering intensified. With a deep, unhappy groan, the tormented stones of Ashdown Castle tore themselves free of the Hyndorin Enclave. We vanished out of the fifth Britain in the blink of an eye.

And arrived in the familiar, deteriorated sixth. Our own, dear, magickal backwater.

I might've preferred to be hit with a sledgehammer.

The way I'd felt in the Other Scarborough — strained, tense, hyperactive, *buzzing* with prickly, stinging energy — was nothing to this. I was eight hundred Vespers crammed into one skin. I was a lit firework, my fuse burning down, explosion imminent. My overwrought brain reeled, my skin burned, my eyes leaked enough tears to fill a small lake.

I could've *made* a small lake, with a flick of my shimmering fingers.

And that was the part I really did not like. The fact that I *did*. Burn though I might in the fires of my own magickal potential, hurt though it did, I didn't want to let it go. I felt as I had in Farringale, when we'd wallowed in our first magickal surge. Only better, because now *I* was in control. *I was the surge.* I could do anything I wanted — at least until I shattered into a thousand pieces.

I'd have welcomed that disintegration rather than voluntarily relinquish all that power.

Vesper, I said in the silence of my fevered mind. *We are in big trouble.*

I PASSED OUT, I suppose. When I was able to wrest my awareness away from the bubbling well of magick taking over my soul, I found myself still in Fenella Beaumont's crummy drawing-room, though I was now receiving a rather different view of it. Too much ceiling.

I lay cradled in Alban's arms, which was humiliating and delicious at the same time. I smiled dreamily up at his dear face, bent over me with so much concern.

'High as a kite,' said Jay from somewhere nearby. 'Don't let go of her, Alban.'

'Never,' he solemnly agreed.

I watched in fascination as Alban's appearance changed before my eyes. His hair, skin and eyes washed through several colours, and he began, gradually, to grow. Then he shrank. Then he grew.

'You're an inconsistent size,' I informed him. 'Sorry.'

He grinned. 'Actually, it's you that's changing.'

'Oh.' I thought, as best I could past the fog in my head. What had happened when I'd hugged Jay, back at the tower? He had absorbed some of my magickal overflow, which had been a good thing at the time.

Alban was now doing the same, and it *wasn't* such a good thing this time. But he was bearing it.

Someone had hold of my wrist, too. I'd thought it was Alban, but when I checked I saw Jay's slim brown fingers wrapped around my hand.

Miranda sat at my feet. She had a grip on my ankle, and she didn't look too pleased about it. But between the three of them, they were siphoning enough off me to keep me in one piece.

'Thanks,' I said.

'Anytime,' said Jay.

I watched for a second as waves of magick pulsed through all three of them, doing some decidedly weird things. I'd really have to get a better grip on all that. I didn't suppose Jay much appreciated growing feathers, though the silvery eye thing was pretty cool.

I looked around.

Em had done something to Fenella. I couldn't tell what, but I did not imagine Ms. Beaumont had taken a seat in Emellana's enormous armchair by choice. She sat with rigidly upright posture, her face fixed in her hostess smile, her hands gripping the chair's tapestried arms. She did not move a muscle.

I caught Em's eye. Somewhere at the back of my mind, beneath the chaos, a feeling of foreboding stirred. Whatever Em had done, it looked eerily like a total subjection of Fenella Beaumont's will. The kind of binding the enchanters of Vale had used upon their unicorns and griffins. The same thing, I suspected, that Fenella had done to both Em and Alban, though with less effect.

Utterly illegal in our Britain, of course.

Emellana met my gaze calmly. Had she winked? Was that my imagination? 'Ves,' she said. 'Help Zareen.'

Again with the helping Zareen? Hadn't I done that enough? I'd already ascertained that Zar was still alive and breathing, which was about as much as I'd hoped for by then. She sat slumped against the wall, white as a sheet, but the blood had ceased to spill from her eyes.

Those eyes, though, were still coal-black, and she was breathing too quickly. 'Yes,' she said, hearing her name, and her gaze settled on me. 'Help me, Ves.'

She spoke far too calmly, under the circumstances, and those eyes gave me the shivers. Nonetheless, I sat up. 'What are we doing?'

'Mass exorcism.'

'Oh.'

She came slowly to her feet, and steadied herself against the wall. 'George was supposed to help me, but since he's otherwise occupied…'

I tried to get a look out of a window. 'Where are we?'

'Back in the castle grounds. And here it shall stay.'

'Make some haste,' said Emellana. 'She is a strong woman. I cannot hold her indefinitely.'

I wanted to just bomb out of there and go Home, but Zareen was right. We had some housekeeping to do.

I held out my hand to Zareen. 'The rest of you had better let go,' I suggested. 'For a bit. Zar gets the lot.'

Alban set me on my feet, and released me, to my distant regret. I focused my attention on Zar, who, with my infusion of raw magick, was rapidly turning scary-as-hell. Again.

And I'm really not kidding. It wasn't just the eyes. She'd been way too pale before, but now she turned stark white in an instant, and sort of ethereal, like she was half-ghost herself. She radiated an icy frigidity, cold as the grave, and my fingers froze in her grip. Magick swirled around us both, ice-cold, smelling of fresh earth and decay.

The bones stood out in Zareen's face. She was half cadaver, a creature of nightmares.

I hung grimly on, and shut my eyes to block out the sight.

But instead of the soothing blackness I'd expected, I received a different vision. I saw — or sensed — the outlines of the castle, magick glimmering in every brick. Shadowed motes blossomed all over the beleaguered place, grave-cold, trailing miasmas of despair. Were these the dead waymasters? I saw why Zareen had been so enraged. Every scrap of light or warmth had been wrested from them; they cowered, shattered and exhausted.

They deserved peace.

But peace was not quite what Zareen delivered. I felt her beside me, radiating icy fury. She was stronger than ever before; *we* were strong. We were one again, for an instant, and she was a queen of the dead as she stretched out her will and took hold of every one of those dark presences.

Then, with the negligent twist of a gardener uprooting a weed, she ripped them free of their earthly bindings and sent them sailing into the void.

With something like a gusty exhalation, Ashdown Castle settled around us, brick by brick, its animating forces dispatched.

'No,' gasped Fenella, twitching. 'My *castle.*' She was moving, slowly but surely, and though Em fought to hold her, she'd lost her grip. Fenella Beaumont, powerful as she was arrogant, wrested herself free of Emellana's magick and surged to her feet. Ignoring Em, her face twisted with fury, she made straight for Zareen — and me.

19

Let it be noted: there are drawbacks to radiating magick like some kind of arcane halogen heater.

It might sound like a good deal, and it certainly has its upsides (see: Zareen's casual exorcism of a ten-strong haunting team, with a flick of her cadaverous fingers).

The downsides, though? For one, it should not be possible for other people to soak up magick like a sponge, just by touching me. It meant I wasn't so much a magickal battery as a broken tap, spewing precious magickal resources every which way with no semblance of control. And if I wasn't in possession of enough hangers-on to take some of the magickal overload, I'd probably burst.

That was really going to play hell with my social life.

For another thing, magick is super fun and all (see: never-ending chocolate pots, and rainbow hair), but it's also scary as hell and dangerous beyond all reason. Give a furious and exhausted woman access to a convenient magickal reservoir, let her be possessed of terrifying necromantic powers, and top it all off by putting her in immediate danger, and... the results are not pretty.

Here's what happened to Fenella Beaumont.

'Shit,' said Zareen, as Fenella rampaged in our direction, wearing the expression of a woman intent on nothing but our total destruction.

It was hard to blame her, even. We did have a regrettable way of wrecking her stuff.

'Do you have *any idea* what you have just done?' she screamed, mostly at Zareen, but her rage certainly included me. '*Ten waymaster spirits!* There probably aren't another ten left in Britain! All that work — what we've expended — the *rarity* — my castle! Ruined!'

I listened, faintly intrigued. I'd never heard anyone literally splutter with fury before.

It occurred to me that I ought to be more worried, but I felt spacy and detached, like I existed on a different magickal plane to everyone else. Perhaps I did.

Zareen, though, was in no way detached. She squared up to Fenella, our own personal Queen of the Dead versus the woman who enslaved spirits, hauled entire castles from world to world, and had built a magickal organisation to rival every other known to man.

They ought to have been evenly matched.

They would have been, if it wasn't for me.

'Stop there,' said Zareen, icy-cold, and her voice boomed and echoed, as though she spoke from the middle of a thunderstorm. Or as though she *was* the thunderstorm.

'Or what?' spat Fenella. 'You've already done your worst.' She whipped out a rose-quartz Wand, and power built around her in waves. Pressure built. Two elemental forces faced off against one another.

'Ves,' hissed Jay, and hands pulled at me. 'You need to get out of here.'

I understood where he was coming from. Any by-standers to this particular fight were likely to end up smashed to smithereens, and I was already in a vulnerable state.

But, leaving Zar to face Fenella's wrath alone was not an option. I shook my head, resisting his — and Alban's — attempts to peel me away.

'My worst?' said Zareen, and smiled. 'Not quite.'

I braced myself for an explosion of some kind, but... nothing happened.

Instead, I felt a faint *woosh*. A small ocean of magick poured out of me; Zareen took it, and with a tilt of her head and a blink of her coal-black eyes, she directed it with devastating force.

Fenella keeled over backwards, and lay inert as a stone.

For about five long seconds, no one spoke.

'You've killed her,' said Jay, and ran to kneel beside Fenella. He peered into her eyes, shook her, and finally checked her pulse. 'She's dead.'

'She is not dead,' said Zareen, and the thunder had yet to fade from her voice.

'Stone dead,' Jay said. 'See for yourself.'

I, drained, slithered to the ground in an inelegant heap. As I released Zareen, the cadaver began to fade from her appearance. Her skin regained a little of its normal colour; flesh returned to her bones, and some of the black drained out of her eyes. She began to shake, but when she spoke again, her words emerged like steel bullets. 'All right, she's temporarily dead.'

'Temporarily?' I said, faintly. 'What did you do to her?'

'Soul-ripped her.' Zareen spoke with awful casualness, and shrugged.

'Which is what—' I began.

Em said, 'Her spirit is separated from her body.' She gestured with one large hand, in a direction slightly removed from Fenella's prone body. 'She is, in ordinary parlance, a ghost.'

'Zar.' I sat up, my head spinning. 'You can't do that to people.'

Zareen gave a faint, huffy sigh. 'I didn't *quite* mean to. It isn't something I *can* do, ordinarily.'

And so I learned that it was my fault. 'Oh,' I said, sagging. 'Sorry.'

'It isn't something anybody can do,' Zareen added, and now she sounded wondering and intrigued. She approached Fenella's body, and eyed the dead woman with interest. 'I'll have to write an essay on it.'

'It is in contravention of at least six magickal laws,' Emellana pointed out.

'Right,' said Zar. 'Maybe not the essay.'

'In the meantime,' said Jay, with emphasis. 'What do we do about it?'

'Do?' Zareen echoed, blinking.

'We can't just leave her like this.'

Zareen shrugged. 'It takes a lot to keep soul and body separate, if the body hasn't actually died. She will soon find her way back. Or George will do it for her.'

'Are you sure the body hasn't died?'

'I didn't *do* anything to it, so I don't see how it would've.' Zareen began to sound annoyed.

And exhausted.

Me, I was losing all the good-in-a-bad-way feelings I'd had, and was coming to feel just plain *bad*. Like I needed to run up a mountain without stopping, and at the same time sleep for about twelve years. 'Um,' I said.

Nobody heard me. An argument flared up between Jay and Zareen, he (not unjustifiably) condemning her for her lack of concern over Fenella's death, she hotly defending her conduct. Emellana, apparently appointing herself as mediator, oversaw the debate; I heard her calm voice chime in from time to time.

It was Alban who picked me up off the floor, where I'd been reclining in a most undignified posture, and steadied me on my feet. 'Are you all right?' he said.

'No,' I whispered, though his touch soothed a little. 'I think... I think I'm going to need Addie.'

'Right.'

'And quickly.'

Here's a little secret.

When I first met Adeline, quite a few years ago, she'd been hanging out in a proper Unicorn Glade situated surprisingly close to Home.

When I say "unicorn glade", I mean that the place was hidden deep inside a tucked-away magickal Dell; it had the full complement of enchanted waters (smelling of nectar), jewel-green grasses, endless sunshine, and singing bees; and its unicorn residents numbered at least five, one of which had been Addie.

No one at Home had ever mentioned there being a Unicorn Glade on the doorstep. Even Milady had never made reference to it, despite knowing all about my friendship with Addie. To this day, I don't know whether that's because it is considered to be a deep, dark secret, or whether no one else actually knows about it.

Anyway, I haven't been back since that one day I went there with the bag of chips, and came out with a new friend. I tried once, but I could not find it again.

Alban got me out of Ashdown Castle. I don't really know how; I wasn't entirely with it, anymore. There was rapid motion as I was swept out into the darkening evening beyond the castle's gates, half-carried by my long-suffering friend, for I was too fascinated by the effects of my overabundant magick to remember quite how to keep putting one foot in front of the other. Every time I took a step, something happened. Flowers bloomed beneath my feet, grew toothy mouths, and tried to bite my ankles. Sparks flew up from the ground, and did their best to set fire to our clothes. I almost drowned in chocolate, when the grass under my feet abruptly turned molten and cocoa-scented, and I had to be hauled out — only to emerge with no trace of chocolate on my shoes.

It went on in this style, proving that while the effects of my peculiar state might be unpredictable and inconsistent, they were certainly going to be persistent. And inconvenient. I definitely heard Alban swearing, at one point.

'Ves,' he said, after a little while, and we stopped. We'd gone far enough away from Ashdown as to be out of sight. 'The pipes? Time to summon Addie.'

'Right.' I dug around in my blouse, fumbling everything with trembling fingers.

Politely, Alban looked away.

'Ha.' I found the pipes, and held them triumphantly aloft. A stray beam of dying sunlight caught them, and they lit up like... well, like a magickal artefact of indescribable power.

'Good,' said Alban, and waited. When I remained where I was, gazing in frozen wonder upon the beauty of my syrinx pipes, he cleared his throat and said: 'Go on. Play them. Play Addie's song.'

I did that. The song got a bit more complicated than usual, as though the pipes were more or less playing themselves. 'Wow,' I said, when I/we had finished. 'I've never been that good!'

Alban grinned. 'You're a mythical creature of limitless power. You'll have to get used to that.'

'That isn't the idea, though, is it?' I said, watching in fascination as the pipes morphed in my hand. 'I'm to be drained of magic, like a wet dish cloth.' The pipes became a conch shell in mother-of-pearl; a magickal Silver thimble;

a miniature kingfisher, clad in gold; a rose the size of my fist, made of pure ruby.

In came Addie with a *swoosh* of her pearly-white wings, and a quadruple *thud* as her silvery hooves hit the turf. She dashed over to me and shoved me with her nose.

'I'm fine,' I lied, and all but fell on her.

She shoved me again, rudely. This wasn't concern. This was anger.

'Fine, I'm sorry,' I babbled. 'I know I took you far away from home, and got you captured by nefarious evil-doers, and then kind of ignored you for a while afterwards—'

She stepped on my foot. I paused to emit a faint shriek.

'—but it isn't that I don't love you,' I gasped, my eyes watering. 'And I don't even have any fried potato products with me to prove it, but I swear I will make up for that, Addie.'

Carefully, Alban extended a hand and patted Addie's silky mane. Under his touch, she calmed maybe just a fraction.

'I need help,' I told her. 'Look.' I held out my left hand to show her. I still *had* a hand, which was nice, only the skin and muscle and bone was gone. I had a jewelled claw of a hand instead, and if I wasn't crazy to even imagine it (always a possibility) I might have said it was wrought out of magickal Silver. My fingernails had a most attractive Silvery sheen.

'This kind of crap is not going to stop,' I said to Addie. 'I also *may* have helped rip a woman into two separate pieces not long ago — physical and incorporeal — and though Zar swears she'll be fine I'm not sure, Addie. I've become a danger, old girl, and I don't like it.' A tear ran down my cheek, turning to something solid on its way down, and fell into the grass in a brief flash of bright gold.

'No one's going to blame you, Ves,' said Alban, reaching for me.

'*I'm* blaming me,' I retorted. 'I may not be at fault for my present condition — it's not like I asked for it — but I am responsible for the outcome.'

'Okay, but still—' said Alban.

'And what kind of a life can I have in this state? I can't even hug a person without turning them into a sodding hippogriff.'

Alban, unable to produce a rational response, merely raised his brows.

'It's happened,' I assured him. 'Well, kind of. At the tower Jay was growing feathers and all that, so I hugged him out of it. But we're all backwards out here, and it isn't that Jay isn't magickal enough for the environment, it's that I am far too much so, so probably the effects will be the other way around too, right?'

'Ves,' said Alban, gently. 'You're stalling.' He looked at me with such heart-melting compassion, I could've cried.

Forget that. I *did* cry, especially when he pushed me gently in Addie's direction. 'She's waiting for you,' he said, and he was right: she'd stopped tossing her head and snorting and stood patiently waiting for me to stop procrastinating and get my act together.

'I'm afraid,' I said, twining my fingers through Addie's mane.

'It will be all right,' said Alban.

Then I was up on Addie's back, and with powerful beats of her wide, beautiful wings, she bore us both up into the skies.

I stared down at Alban's big, big frame as he dwindled to dwarfish proportions beneath us, and then vanished altogether. He was waving.

'Take me somewhere safe, Addie,' I pleaded, and buried my face in her mane.

She took me to her Glade. We came down softly in a carpet of thick moss, cool beneath my feet in the gathering twilight. I smelled nectar and fresh grass, and heard the soothing ripple of running water somewhere near.

I calmed at once, for the magick of Addie's Glade had a depth to it; an ancient potency which somehow soothed the runaway chaos inside me. I stamped once, flicking an ear, as the night-time sounds of the peaceful Dell seemed to jump into sharper focus.

A dulcet breeze swept back my mane, and starlight glittered off the tip of my horn.

'Addie!' I called, for she was trotting away from me. The sound emerged as a penetrating *whicker*. 'Wait for me!'

She looked back over her shoulder, one ear pointed straight up, and whickered back. *Hurry up, then.*

I hurried.

20

Some unknowable time later, I was dozing by the lily-pool when an unusual scent caught my nostrils.

I lifted my head, so fast as to crack my crown against the low-hanging branches above me. I snorted in annoyance.

Addie pretended she hadn't noticed, but I could tell by her studiedly serene posture that she had. *And* she was laughing at me.

'*Addie*!' I hissed. 'Do you smell that?'

She lifted her nose, and inhaled.

Then she bolted up right, and shot away from the pool at a full gallop.

I followed at a (slightly) more sedate pace, laughing.

I caught up with her at the mouth of our perfect little glade. She had her rump turned to me, her tail swishing, nose-down in a bag of chips. I poked my nose over her shoulder to have a look. They were the fat-cut kind, her favourite. Crispy on the outside, pillowy in the middle, and translucent with grease.

The bag was held by Jay.

'Okay, this one's Adeline,' he called, and I saw somebody else behind him. Somebody tall, and broad-shouldered, with green-tinted skin, emerald-bright eyes, and bronzed, artfully-windswept hair.

My nose informed me that he, too, had brought an of-fering.

I swarmed past Addie and almost knocked the Baron over in my enthusiasm. Whether it was his presence that awoke such feelings, or the enormous plate he carried in his hands, I couldn't have said. I mean, that sounds bad, but he'd brought *pancakes.* Not just any pancakes, either, but troll-sized pancakes; the kind we'd eaten that day at breakfast, when he had taken me out on what turned out to not be a date.

Well, at least the pancakes had been good. *Seriously* good. And these were the same: dripping in syrup, laden with ice cream, and tooth-achingly sweet.

I was halfway down the plate before it occurred to me to wonder what they were doing in our Glade, or how they had found it.

'So we've found Ves,' said Jay, laughing.

Alban winced, and steadied himself, almost bowled over by my attack on the pancake plate.

That was new. I, scrawny Ves, was big and muscly enough to knock over a troll.

'Ves?' said Alban. 'That *is* you, isn't it?'

I lifted my head, chewing an enormous mouthful of crisp pancake batter and mixed-fruit ice cream. 'Obviously?' I said, spraying syrup.

The word emerged as a whinny.

'Damnit,' I sighed. Another whinny.

'It has to be Ves,' said Jay. 'You sent her off with Addie, and Addie's here. How likely is it that there are two pancake-obsessed unicorns living on the Society's doorstep?'

'Obsessed?' I objected. 'I'm not *obsessed*. I can stop anytime I want.' I punctuated this statement with an emphatic gulp of sweet, delicious food, and then took a determined step back, shaking my head.

This was *real* heroism, I thought, mournfully eyeing the plate. Forget precision-strike raids on ancient magickal towers, and wresting vital magickal history out of the proverbial grave. Refraining from eating the last mouthfuls of pancakes and ice cream? That was the stuff of legend.

'Fine, I take it back,' said Jay, grinning. 'You aren't in the least bit obsessed with pancakes.'

I nodded my satisfaction, made a lunge for the plate, and swallowed the last morsels in two bites.

'Right, so,' said Jay, patting my neck. 'We've found Ves. Now what?'

Alban set the plate down in the grass, and I devoted myself to licking it clean of every last drop of syrup. 'Milady said to bring her in, no?'

'I have no idea how we're going to get her up all those stairs.'

'Maybe House can help with that.'

'Might do,' Jay agreed. Then he added, 'Come to think of it, I have no idea how we're going to get her out of this glade.'

'She does look comfortable,' Alban agreed.

I beamed. I *was* comfortable. 'I was born to be a unicorn,' I informed them both.

'Uh huh.' Jay looked a little wide-eyed as he stared at me. 'I possibly don't want to know what you just said.'

I bumped Addie with my shoulder, rubbed my nose against her side, and waited. If I stood here and looked pretty, would someone show up with more pancakes? This approach had been working pretty well for Addie.

'You want to come with us, Ves?' said Jay. 'Milady wants to see you.'

I twitched my tail, thinking it over. Or, I tried. Memories slipped away like the water-weeds I'd tried to eat from the lily pond. I knew these men; they were dear to me. But they belonged to another time, one that faded like a dream whenever I tried to fix my thoughts upon it.

Stray memories of chocolate-pots and endless stairs floated through my mind; of velvet-clad wingback chairs, and heavy piles of books; of a huge desk in a huge library, Val sitting behind it; of a long avenue of trees, sometimes upside-down, and Zareen with a poison-green streak in her hair.

'I don't know,' I said, licking syrup from my lips. 'It's peaceful here.'

'Come on,' said Jay. 'Please? The Society needs you.'

I snorted.

'We need you,' added Jay.

'True,' said Alban. 'We do. Pup's lost without you. Val told me she'd chop off your horn if you didn't come home. And Zareen sent this.' He held up his phone. Letters on the screen swam about a bit, and came into focus: *Ves, get your sorry butt back Home or you'll be SORRY.*

My ear twitched. Nobody wanted to get in the Queen of the Dead's bad books.

'The thing is,' I said, sidling about a bit. 'I don't seem to have any hands.'

Jay sighed. 'I wish we knew what she was saying.'

'Or feet,' I continued. 'Or arms. You can't be much of an agent without a few things like that, and I've kind of lost mine.'

Jay and Alban blinked blankly at me.

'Do you happen to know how to de-horn me?' I said. '*Not* in the way Val said. Do you have any idea how to make me Ves-shaped and humanoid? Because damned if I do.' I wasn't altogether sure I wanted to be Ves-shaped and humanoid again; I had the vague but settled sense that I had been making a right royal mess of being Ves, lately. I'd been okay as a unicorn. I was *good* as a unicorn.

'Why don't you just come with us?' said Jay. 'And we'll see what happens? Nod once for yes. Shake for no.'

I stamped a foot.

'Is that yes?' said Jay.

I gave a horsie sigh, nipped affectionately at Addie's neck, and stomped off towards the Glade's entrance.

'Ooh, we're going,' said Jay, and ran after me.

I left the Glade with a dual escort, Jay's hand resting on the left side of my neck, Alban's hand upon my right. I felt fine. I felt *great*.

Only, once we were over the threshold, every-thing fell apart. The lovely, fizzy feeling of mag-ick-down-to-my-bones faded away, and with it, my flow-ing, shampoo-advertisement mane. When I tossed my head, the satisfying *thwoosh* of my horn slicing through empty air abruptly disappeared. I put up a hand, and groped around atop my own head.

'Damnit,' I sighed. 'Did it have to be that easy...?'

'Welcome back, Ves,' said Jay, and I waited in general expectation of being hugged by somebody.

It didn't happen. My gentleman companions were, if anything, edging away from me.

'Oh, come on. I don't get a welcome-back-to-two-legged-kind squish?'

'Clothes,' Jay coughed.

I looked down.

There weren't any.

'It did feel a bit draughty out here,' I said nonchalantly. 'Anybody lend me a something?'

Jay looked helplessly at Alban. Here in the height of summer, nobody needed coats much, and neither of them was wearing one. A jaunty sun bathed us in such balmy warmth, I wouldn't have minded proceeding without clothes, except that I was clearly making my gentlemen uncomfortable.

'Alban,' I said, beaming. 'I could wear your shirt like a dress.'

I could, too. The hem would probably hit me somewhere around mid-thigh, which was enough to preserve modesty until I could pick up some of my own clothes.

My request had nothing whatsoever to do with a desire to see a certain dishy troll without his shirt. Honest.

'All right,' said Alban, and my heart leapt.

But instead of stripping off his white, long-sleeved shirt, he plucked at it with both hands, and made a peeling motion. Another shirt came away in his hands, identical to the first. He shook this second shirt out, and gave it to me.

'Nice trick,' I said, and put it on. It might not be Alban's real shirt (I guess?), but it was still faintly warm from his skin. I rolled up the sleeves a bit more.

'I don't have a lot of magick,' said Alban, with a wry smile. 'And I can't do anything useful with it. But sartorial quandaries I can certainly solve.'

'My hero,' said I, and Jay rolled his eyes.

'WELCOME BACK, VES,' SAID Milady a little later.

I'd been delivered up to her tower by my joint escort, and they had left me there for a no-doubt minute debriefing. I'd dived past my own room on the way up, and grabbed a summer dress out of my wardrobe, plus a pair of sandals. It wouldn't do to present oneself before Milady in nothing but a borrowed man's shirt. I'd also found my shoulder-bag lying upon my bed, with all my stuff in it. No Mauf, though.

'How long was I gone?' I asked.

'About three weeks.'

'That's… longer than I thought.'

'And how did you enjoy your sojourn among the unicorns?'

'It's like I was one of them.'

'Indeed.' The air sparkled with her mirth. 'Do you feel… in health?'

'You mean, am I still an out-of-control magickal fountain, causing chaos wherever I go? No. I think… I think I'm okay.'

And I was. I still fizzed oddly with magick from time to time, and I couldn't absolutely swear that weird things wouldn't happen around me once in a while. But I felt more… centred. Less like a storm in a teacup. More like the old Ves. Kind of.

My bond with Addie, formed through the unusual and unexpected expedient of adopting her shape, her lifestyle and her company for three long weeks, held strong even when I was back in my regular configuration. I felt it, close to my heart, an invisible link across which magick flowed like the cool waters of the lily stream.

'The Glade is a safe repository for the excess,' said Milady with approval. 'It is fortunate that you were able to bond with Adeline.'

'Fortunate,' I agreed, thinking of all the "fortunate" things that tended to happen around Milady. I hovered on the brink of asking her about my clairvoyance theory, and... didn't. Did I lack the courage?

Apparently.

'The lyre has been delivered back to your mother,' Milady continued. 'Jay has submitted a full report of its effects upon you. This is under investigation.'

'Great.'

'You may also like to know that Miranda is back with the Society.'

'Ah...?'

'She has not yet been restored to her former privileges and position, but I have hopes that this may come to pass in time.'

I said nothing.

'Do you disapprove, Ves?'

'I don't trust her,' I said bluntly.

'We will all need time to rebuild our trust.'

'Hmph.' I swallowed my disgruntlement, and set the matter aside. Milady, invariably, knew best. 'What about Torvaston's research?'

'Ah! Yes! You are all to be congratulated for such an exciting discovery. Your book — Gallimaufry — is with the library at present; Valerie is consulting him regarding the various records and copies he was able to make during your mission. Jay's pictures also. The Court, meanwhile, has been loud in its praise of you all. They are extremely pleased with the results you were able to produce.'

'Cool,' I said. 'And?'

'I don't precisely understand the question.'

'Are we building a new Heart of Hyndorin?'

'The Court appears to favour the term *magickal modulator.*'

'Snappy. How nicely it alliterates.'

'Quite. It is not yet known whether we will be able to recreate Torvaston's work, but naturally we are prepared to try. Once the plans have been suitably processed, studied and stored, they will be delivered to Orlando. The Court will also be sending us one or two of their own inventors, to assist with the work.'

'We do seem to be forging close links with the Court these days.'

'Our goals happen to align.'

I fiddled with my own fingers, and shifted from foot to foot.

'What is it, Ves?' said Milady.

'Can I come Home?' I blurted. 'Can *we* come home? It's been wild working for the Court, but...' I couldn't put my homesickness into words, and I didn't try. Milady must know how I felt.

'I believe the project may now be declared out of your hands,' said Milady. 'There is no need for any repeat missions to the fifth Britain at this time.'

'And if the Ministry takes exception to the pursuit of Torvaston's project, we're calling it Mandridore's fault?'

'It is entirely their fault,' said Milady serenely.

'Does that mean yes?'

'Yes, Ves, I think it does.'

I fist-bumped the empty air.

'Though,' said Milady. 'You will find that Zareen is not presently in residence.'

'Is she all right?'

'She is in poor health. I have sent her for treatment.'

Probably she had gone back to the School of Weird, or some related facility. My heart twisted with regret. Poor Zar had taken a serious beating; worse than the rest of us. Had it been worth it?

'I believe she will make a full recovery,' added Milady. 'But it will be some time before she will rejoin us.'

'Soooo,' I said, smiling in sheer relief. 'Everybody's okay.'

'More or less.'

'And we're all Home. Or will be.'

'I hope that you will all remain so.'

'What's my next assignment, Boss?'

'Take some rest.'

I blinked. 'That's not very fun.'

'But it is necessary. You are almost as much in need of restful recovery as Zareen.'

'No way. I've had three weeks in unicorn paradise. I'm fine.'

'Rest,' said Milady firmly. 'After which, I will have an exciting new job for you.'

My ears pricked up at that. 'Ohhh?'

'I cannot share too many details at present, but—'

'Come *on*,' I pleaded. 'Don't leave me in suspense!'

'Well. If Orlando, and his team, conclude that a new modulator may be successfully created from Torvaston's plans, then of course the Court will put such a project into immediate development.'

'Yes!'

'And that means that materials will be required.'

'Materials... oooh. You mean magickal Silver.'

'What the Yllanfalen refer to as moonsilver. Yes.'

'Or skysilver. I can never remember which. Is that what we're calling it?'

'I think "suitable materials" will suffice.'

'I suppose it's as good a code word as any.'

'As you must be aware, this kind of *suitable material* is in short supply,' said Milady firmly, towing us back on track.

'Yes. It's supposed to be mined out, even on the fifth.'

'I believe we can conclude that there are no more accessible, naturally-occurring sources of this material remaining.'

'Maybe on one of the other Britains?'

'There is little reason to think so. And if there were, I cannot in the least imagine how we would find them. Can you?'

'Well... no. There— did Jay tell you? There is a stash of it in Torvaston's tower.'

'Yes, but he is not of the opinion that it would be possible, or indeed desirable, to try to take it.'

He had a point. Luan would never give it up willingly, certainly not for such a purpose. The Earl strongly disapproved of the whole idea of recreating Torvaston's invention. And to flat-out steal it... no. We, the Society, were better than that. We had to be.

'I do have another idea,' said Milady.

I perked up. 'Is this one of your hunchy-things?'

'My what?'

I coughed. 'Er, nothing.'

There was a slight pause.

'The fact is,' Milady resumed. 'I have consulted Val.'

'Always a good move!'

'She reports the existence of one or two ancient resources which suggest an interesting alternative. It may no longer be possible to pull natural Silver out of the ground, but if history is to be believed, one or two individuals have undertaken serious attempts to create it.'

'Alchemy?' I blurted.

'Exactly.'

'But— but— alchemy's a dead art. Nobody's bothered with transmutation in years.'

'No one has *publically* attempted alchemical transmutation in years,' Milady corrected.

'You know I'm a sucker for a nice, dark secret.'

'Indeed. Let me worry about *who* is going to perform this transmutation. Your job is to discover the means.'

'I'm on the hunt for a long-lost recipe?'

'Yes. I want you and Val to find out if these documents are authentic, and their accounts reliable. If they are, then your next task is to unearth further resources.'

My heart performed a weird flutter of excitement. Library mission! Yes!

'So,' I said. 'When you say "rest"...'

'If some part of this period of recovery involves your spending time in the library, I shall be quite satisfied.'

'Attended, perhaps, by a duvet and a pot of chocolate?' I said hopefully.

'I believe that will be acceptable.'

I whipped out my phone, now blessedly functional again. *Val,* I typed. *Weeks-long library slumber party. You and me. Starting now.*

'I'll get right on that,' I told Milady.

The air sparkled again. 'I thought you might.'

My phone buzzed. Message from Val. It said: *Get down here, slowpoke.*

I kicked up my heels, and got going.

Milady spoke once more as I wrenched open the tower door. 'Ves?' she called. 'There's chocolate in the pot.'

Also By Charlotte E. English

Modern Magick

The Road to Farringale

Toil and Trouble

The Striding Spire

The Fifth Britain

Royalty and Ruin

Music and Misadventure

The Wonders of Vale

The Heart of Hyndorin

Alchemy and Argent
The Magick of Merlin
Dancing and Disaster

House of Werth

Wyrde and Wayward
Wyrde and Wicked
Wyrde and Wild

www.ingramcontent.com/pod-product-compliance
Lightning Source LLC
LaVergne TN
LVHW040008200726
843493LV00005B/1176